In a Valley of
this Restless Mind

In a Valley of
this Restless Mind

MALCOLM
MUGGERIDGE

Illustrations by Papas

COLLINS
St James's Place, London
1978

48086

William Collins Sons & Co Ltd
London · Glasgow · Sydney · Auckland
Toronto · Johannesburg

First published by George Routledge & Sons Ltd in 1938
First published by William Collins Sons & Co Ltd, 1978
© Malcolm Muggeridge 1938, 1978
Illustrations © Papas, 1978

ISBN 0 00 216337 3

Set in Baskerville
Made and printed in Great Britain by
William Collins Sons & Co Ltd Glasgow

Contents

Introduction

I find it very hard to read anything I have written once it has appeared in print. This is probably a consequence of years of journalism spent writing for newspapers and periodicals whose lives, apart from the files of back numbers, are necessarily brief. It gives one an engrained sense that all words are transitory, whether in a daily, a weekly, a monthly or between hard covers; today featured, tomorrow used to wrap fish or light fires, or just pulped. Thus, after the publication of *In a Valley of this Restless Mind* in 1938, I felt little inclined to turn over its pages, and during the succeeding forty years have only very rarely remembered its existence, though I have to acknowledge a few devoted readers who have continued to hold it in esteem, among them my son John, and Professor Ian Hunter of the University of Western Ontario, to whom I am greatly beholden for having been an indefatigable collector of my writings. Now, four decades later, confronted with a new edition superbly illustrated by Papas, I still find difficulty in recognizing the book as my own true progeny.

The book was commissioned in the first place by Jonathan Cape via an old friend, Rupert Hart-Davis, then on Cape's staff. The intention – my own suggestion – was to produce a systematic study of contemporary religious attitudes and practices, rather in the manner of William James's famous work, *Varieties of Religious Experience*. What I turned in was so outrageously different from the original concept that, understandably, it proved to be unacceptable. Later, another publisher – Routledge – agreed to publish the book as it stood, and it duly appeared in 1938. My failure to carry out the original assignment – something that has happened on numerous occasions, I regret to say – was partly at any rate due to a deep distaste I have had all my life for what passed for being facts and a profound scepticism about their validity. This attitude of mind may well have been fostered by the three unprofitable years I spent at Cambridge ostensibly

7

reading for a Natural Science Tripos. The old Roman practice of using the entrails of a chicken to forecast the future has always seemed to me more realistic than Dr Gallup's procedures, and I have come to regard the computer, next only to the camera, as the most sinister of all contemporary inventions. The point was made very cogently by the late A. T. Cholerton, *Daily Telegraph* correspondent in Moscow at the time of the Stalinist purges in the early Thirties, when some visiting liberal *exalté* asked whether the evidence offered at the trials of the Old Bolsheviks was reliable. 'Everything is true,' Cholerton replied magisterially, 'except the facts.'

Seeing facts as the supreme fantasy was clearly not conducive to producing another *Varieties of Religious Experience* – something, incidentally, still requiring to be done. Instead, there was this rambling, introspective, egocentric twentieth century *Pilgrim's Progress*, or rather, as one reviewer suggested, *Pilgrim's Regress*. I did in point of fact make some desultory attempts to unearth what might pass for being documentary material, of which there are traces in the book. For instance, I actually attended a revivalist meeting in the Albert Hall, went to breakfast with an archdeacon with a view to questioning him about God, spent some time with Father Boniface at his monastery, encountered Mrs Angel along the Embankment, dropped in on Wilberforce at his office when he was engaged in writing a leading article and consulted Dr Appleblossom. Furthermore, all the characters in the book without exception are real people, most of whom I can still identify. In one or two cases where my memory failed me, Papas's illustrations have served to remind me of the originals, which is a great compliment to his skill as an illustrator. None of this, however, sufficed to turn what is essentially a dream, or maybe nightmare, into what sociologists call a study.

In terms of time, *In a Valley* belongs to the nebulous period of waiting for the inevitable outbreak of the 1939-45 war. A sort of lost weekend of history, spent largely with a crystal radio set and wearing earphones, haunted by

Neville Chamberlain's lugubrious voice and the twin tragi-comedies of the Abdication and the Nazi-Soviet Pact. No doubt something of the general atmosphere has seeped into the narrative. People of my age group – mid-thirties – mostly expected to die in the much-prophesied holocaust when it came, paying the death they felt they had somehow defaulted on twenty years before. I, on the contrary, was afflicted with a special dread lest, despite everything, I continued to live. Death in battle seemed too easy an option, as indeed it proved to be. For I was not to die. Nor, for that matter, were the great majority of those who had so unctuously prepared themselves for death. In the event, they were fated to be aspiring rather than actual casualties; fodder in search of cannons, sacrificial offerings which were hard to place, leftovers from the previous war – the Kaiser's – who never found a place in Hitler's. The predicament has been brilliantly described in Evelyn Waugh's War Trilogy, and needs no further exposition.

Obviously, if I were writing *In a Valley* today, I should do it differently. It was even a temptation, in preparing the text for republication, to make alterations and excisions. The obsession with carnality, looked back on across four decades, could not but seem distasteful, especially as I have often criticized other writers for indulging this particular obsession. Yet to have altered and adjusted the text to conform better with present attitudes would have been cheating; if the book was worth republishing at all, I decided, it could only be exactly as I wrote it at the time. No doubt St Augustine would have been well content to omit parts of his *Confessions*, but thereby the total effect of this great work would have been much diminished. We cannot sub-edit our lives; the totality is all. So, nothing has been altered or omitted; the narrator, whom I must regretfully acknowledge to be myself, has been left to go wandering about the streets of London weighed down by his burden of Lust as Bunyan's Pilgrim was by his burden of Sin. I daresay their burdens were not all that dissimilar; Sin has as many varieties as Heinz beans, but the essential ingredients tend to be always the same. The Devil, a con-man of con-men, finds the same old formula goes on working from generation to generation and from age to age.

Of the Seven Deadly Sins, Lust is the only one which makes any serious appeal to the Imagination, as distinct from the Will, eroticism being a sort of *ersatz* transcendentalism which can easily be mistaken for the genuine article. It is easy to say, as contemporary moralists frequently do, that sins of the flesh are less heinous than those of the ego; even easier to transfer the whole issue from the individual to the collectivity, and in denouncing racial prejudice, or imperial arrogance, or economic exploitation with much sound and fury, to let Lust slip away unnoticed. No one, anyway, can accuse my narrator of falling into this particular error; he wears his Lust like a millstone round his neck, while exemplifying, as he was meant to, the truth of the Apostle Paul's saying that to be carnally minded is death and to be spiritually minded life and peace. In his notice of *In a Valley* Evelyn Waugh deals with the Lust *motif* very perceptively. After suggesting that the book has affinities with *Candide* in form and with *Voyage au bout de la nuit* in temper, he goes on:

> Several incidents illustrate the author's attitude to Lust, which is that of the surfeited and rather scared Calvinist. No one with an acute moral sense could take these passages for pornography; they will, however, be distasteful to those who shirk the theological implications of the word 'Lust'; to those, in particular, who like something 'spicey'. They are very dry and gloomy episodes reminiscent of the 'When lovely woman stoops to folly' passage in *The Waste Land*. In brief, what the author has discovered and wishes to explain is the ancient piece of folk-wisdom that Lust and Love are antithetical and that Lust is boring.

I can only say of this passage that no author could hope to

have his intentions more luminously expressed and expounded.

It came as a surprise to me to find the narrator in *In a Valley* has three different names – Motley, Wraithby and Flammonde; if this was planned when I wrote the book, it has quite escaped my memory. Motley I take to be after lines in one of Shakespeare's sonnets that I often say over to myself:

> Alas, 'tis true I have been here and there
> And made myself a motley to the view,

leading up to the brave but unconvincing resolution:

> Mine appetite I never more will grind.

Wraithby is a name I've often assumed myself in a variety of contexts, fictional and non-fictional. Flammonde occurs in an endearingly fatuous couplet by the American poet Edwin Arlington Robinson:

> And women young and old were fond
> Of looking at the man Flammonde.

Was there perhaps some unconscious purpose in thus making my narrator a threefold anchorman, comprehending Motley the womanizer, Wraithby the anti-hero and Flammonde the returned traveller from over the hill; three strands in contemporary fraudulance, and an awful warning of the danger of venturing into the Valley of the Shadow of Life?

By the time *In a Valley* was actually published the coming war was getting very near, so that the book made its appearance as a sort of incorrigible civilian in a world in uniform, a Displaced Book with nowhere to go. I cannot remember being much concerned about its reception, being in any case engrossed myself in completing a book on the Thirties before hostilities began. To provide the necessary data I had purchased a complete set of *The Times* covering the decade, and these were arranged in piles round the room I was working in, literally walling me in. It was a scene very much in the vein of *In a Valley*, which might perfectly well have been subtitled *Studies in Fearful Symmetry*. Whether I was really as unconcerned as I now suppose about how the book fared, I cannot be sure. Anyway, I certainly saw it as being in a category of its own, and felt that it would turn out to be either some sort of weird masterpeice or a fiasco. And that is very much how I feel about it still. My last glimpse of the book was, metaphorically speaking, on the night of the great fires in the City during the London Blitz, which I happened to witness from St James's Park. As the flames consuming the unsold and unremaindered stock of publishers in the warehouses along Paternoster Row, including residual copies of *In a Valley*, leapt into the sky, I could reflect sardonically that, among other amazing feats, war had at last made me a best seller. Contrary to expectations, *In a Valley* had, after all, helped set the Thames on fire.

Whatever may have been my feelings about the book, I did go to the trouble of pasting up the various notices of it as they appeared, and I have them still, yellowing and fading, sometimes with a smudged picture of the author as he then was. Rather sad trophies, actually; some of the publications in which they appeared long since defunct, and a good many of the reviewers likewise, but the tone mostly sympathetic, and occasionally ecstatic. The one that interested me most was naturally Waugh's, which was quite long and appeared in the *Spectator*. I had always assumed we should be in different camps, and his warm praise of the book surprised and delighted me. During the war I found myself sitting next to him on a bench at a party given by the Duff-Coopers on an archeological site outside Algiers, and attempted to thank him. The attempt was a failure; nothing came of our encounter, and now he, too, is dead. It would be rather silly and pretentious to add a dedication to *In a Valley*, but were I to do so it would be to Evelyn Waugh, who understood what I meant as I think I understand what he meant, with deep esteem and admiration for what he failed to be and do.

It is generally assumed, by those who know me only through the media, especially television, that for the greater part of my life my attitudes were wholly hedonistic and my ways wholly worldly, until, in my sixties, I suddenly discovered God and became preoccupied with other-worldly considerations. *In a Valley*, written all those years ago, confutes this view, which is, for me, a special reason for rejoicing at its reappearance. The fact is that, unlike Demas, I have never cared much for this present world, and have found its pleasures and prizes, such as they are, little to my taste even in pursuing them. *In a Valley*, if it says anything, says this – that it is only to see through the world that we live in the world; only in seeking for the peace it cannot give, for the freedom that is unattainable in it, that we can grasp the peace of God that passes understanding and the glorious liberty of the children of God, the only enduring freedom there is. I wish I had said it better, more convincingly, more beautifully, more positively – like John Henry Newman:

> When a man discerns in himself most sin and humbles himself most, when his comeliness seems to him to vanish away and all his graces to wither, when he feels disgust at himself, and revolts at the thought of himself – seems to himself all dust and ashes, all foulness and odiousness, then it is that he is really rising in the Kingdom of God.

A clearer, greener, better signposted Valley, but still likewise a Valley of a Restless Mind.

Malcolm Muggeridge

13

I

The Cross

Looking for God, I sat in Westminster Abbey and watched sightseers drift by. The Cross on the altar was covered with grey cloth, like chairs at spring-cleaning. It had survived much in two thousand years and inspired much. Many scenes had been enacted in its shadow, and many eyes looked up at it in hope or despair. Thinking of it now my heart melted, I scarcely knew why. Even covered with grey cloth, and with sightseers shuffling to and fro and whispering, it was poignant, seeming to promise an alternative to the Will's arrogance, the Flesh's passion, and Time's inevitable corruption.

'A gibbet,' my father used to say of it, 'and I hate gibbets.'

He disapproved of capital punishment and so of Christ's crucifixion. Yet when he set up his frail platform to speak at a street corner among people and traffic, shadowed against the evening sky, arms outstretched and eyes tormented, it might have been a crucifixion.

The sightseers looked about them curiously, up at the vaulted roof and at statues and inscriptions registering the Dead. They whispered questions:

'Are the Tombs of the Kings free today?'

'Not free.'

'What is free, then? Only the nave, I suppose.'

Some of them, ticketed, clung forlornly together, like sheep, a shepherd conducting them and whispering shrill instructions.

Worshipping a gibbet was like a thirsty Saviour gulping his vinegar. 'Is there,' I wondered, 'no more in resignation than acceptance? Is death the only peace that passes understanding? Must appetite be lulled and coaxed to sleep like a restless child, or burn out in anguish?'

Once I sat at a long white table, ink-stained, watching

15

a road wind up a hill among trees. Evening came, the day spent, its business done. So much cooler my blood, so much drier my skin and greyer my hair; so much cooler the earth and the sun and the stars, and the universe imperceptibly nearing its end, as I was.

It was a lull, like when the press of customers in a shop momentarily ceases, and the shop-assistants, all day long pushing packages into outstretched hands and receiving money in exchange, are able to pause and be at ease for a little while. I sat at this long ink-stained table thinking of my life, and wondering how it had come to pass and what it signified, until shrill voices, my own and another, broke the silence –

'You don't love me any more.'

'I do love you.'

'No.'

'I've seen beyond love.'

'A trick.'

Was it a trick? – happiness learning sorrow, ecstasy learning resignation, corporeal learning incorporeal, the Flesh dying and the Soul rising out of its ashes. Was the Cross a trick, twenty centuries old, and still being played; there in front of me, wrapped in grey cloth?

The sightseers went away to eat, and I remained. It was quiet and still. The House of God, I thought; so many Houses of God, with bell and altar and stained-glass windows. If there was no God to dwell in these Houses how desolate they were! I looked round for God. The brass eagle bearing an opened Bible was inanimate, and the vaulted stone roof leaden as a wintry sky. Oh for an unforgettable vision, the Cross glowing within its grey cover, the brass eagle raising its wings, the stone roof unfolding to disclose God seated in the Heavens among His angels. Oh for a Comforter coming in the likeness of a dove, or a tongue of fire sprouting from my forehead.

I sat on uncomforted. 'Blessed are the pure in heart for they shall see God,' I thought, and prayed: 'Purify me, purify me.' If my heart was pure, I should see God. Swept and garnished, my heart provided a habitation for other demons; other demons chained, its own multiplied. I stank and the World stank, and yet I was to sweeten the World and the World to sweeten me. The Cross remained unillumined, the brass eagle inanimate, the stone vaulted roof did not unfold, nor any dove descend, nor any tongue of flame sprout from my forehead.

A little clearing had been made, as in a street accident. Nine million pressed round, elbowing, standing on tiptoe to see over each other's shoulders, and I sat alone, praying, 'Purify me, purify me.' To this little clearing living shoulders bore the illustrious Dead. The past accumulated here in dust, each century leaving its deposit. It was like Eternity, and outside Time rumbled by, I with it. It was like sleep, and outside dreams of love and hate, of desire and satiety.

2

Through Interminable Streets

I hurried through interminable streets. Hawkers made meaningless noises, and passing faces were incomprehensible. Wax figures stared at me from shop windows, and my face was warmed with sudden gusts of food-flavoured air. Inside my clothes my body became rank, like damp hay left in the sun. Fresh fruit was piled on barrows, and an old man sang for pennies in a quavering voice: –

> Dearest, I am growing old
> Silver hairs among the gold.

Pursuing and pursued, I hurried on, reading in mauve letters, 'Famous Singer Dead,' thirsting because a paper glass was held to paper lips, reaching after paper flesh, counting over paper riches and fearful of paper destitution. Chaos enfolded me like petals, and at the heart myself, a Chaos. I was drowning in Chaos, sick with salty gulps of it. Shapes formed in my mind, passing across it like the shadows of clouds across a lake. This was Man as producer, pigs jostling round a trough; this Man as reproducer, burying a piece of his body in another body, emerging from a belly's darkness into the light of the sun: –

> My mother groaned, my father wept,
> Into the dangerous world I leapt.

This was Man humble, likening himself to grass one day growing and the next cast into the oven, and this Man arrogant, abolishing the past and decreeing the future.

Now the streets changed. They were frailer and more fantastic. Houses were planted like flowers in a bed, all new, and women in bright dresses passed in and out of their doors, and music played. 'Mansions of light and love,' I thought;

'pleasant arbours made for the refreshing of weary travellers.'
I knocked at a coloured door and waited, footsteps stirring within.

'No hawkers, no canvassers,' a woman said severely, opening the door. 'It's on the gate.'

I had nothing to sell and nothing to canvass. 'Would you be so kind,' I said, 'as to direct me to the nearest church.'

She looked at me suspiciously, slim and grey-skirted, mouth a red compressed line, cheek-bones prominent.

'There's a Congregational Chapel at the end of the road, and a Church of England third on the right.'

As she made to shut the door I asked hurriedly, 'Do many people go to them?'

'Not many, I think,' she answered, relenting. 'We're Scientists. At least I am. My husband hasn't joined but comes with me sometimes to meetings.'

'Has it made you pure of heart?' I asked eagerly.

'I read and thought a lot before I joined, of course.' Her voice dropped. 'I had a trouble. I thought I might go mad.'

The frail, coloured house darkened. The roses growing in a circular bed twisted into a little sinister jungle. The coloured curtains in the bay windows made ominous shadows.

'Then I realized there was no evil in the world, no disease, no pain.' She looked defiantly across the street and repeated as she shut the door, 'No evil, no disease, no pain.'

The Congregational Chapel along the road was shut and deserted, and the Church of England third on the right needed funds for its completion. It was getting dark. Lights came out one by one like stars. Passers-by were shadowy, and separate sounds merged into a confused murmur. Evil and disease and pain had been abolished. Where was there Evening Thanksgiving? From the railway station people came thronging, and then scattered. Where was their place of worship? Where did they gather together and lift up their hearts?

I found a queue and joined it. We progressed slowly forward, huddled in the darkness and moving towards light. Now the radiance caught our faces. We were shining and

transfigured, on the very threshold of a Heavenly City. Carpets softened our footfall, and angels in purple and gold guided our way. There was music in the distance. The air was full of fragrance and sweet airs. At a little aperture each of us paused to pay. Supposing like Ignorance I should fumble in my bosom for my Certificate and find none. Thankfully I clutched a coin in my fingers, passed it in at the aperture, heard its joyous ring, and entered.

Reposing in red plush I had heavenly visions. I saw all that I desired, not to torment me, but abstracted and cool, passing in light and shadow across a screen. I was rich without anxiety and poor without privation; I succeeded without sacrilege and failed without regrets; I loved without apprehension and renounced without despair. Ageless, I exulted in youth; lustless, I tore shimmering dresses from white bodies. From a high mountain I saw all the Kingdoms of the Earth and the glory of them, and they were mine both to accept and discard. Flesh tingled as I lolled on red plush. Eyes watered, mouth indolently smiled. As the vision ended a shining organ rose and hung suspended, and all our pent-up thankfulness burst forth in song. We sang to the organ's accompaniment a rapturous hymn of praise: –

> I'd give my all
> In answer to your call
> For a night of paradise.

I walked away along cold silent streets. Snow began to fall, obliterating the day that had ended, muffling footsteps and traffic. Soon the streets were deserted. Even the houses seemed asleep. I was alone in a white silent city, my faint footprints covered as soon as made. Lifeless the dark buildings, unread the posters and electric signs calling me to hunger and thirst and lust; the Famous Singer really dead at last, evil and disease and pain at last really abolished. Alone, all alone, I again looked round for God, up at the lowering sky, down at the white pavement, in my bewildered soul. 'Purify me, purify me,' I groaned, my voice echoing and re-echoing like a forlorn traveller's, lost in an arctic desert, and was suddenly glad. How lovely the untouched snow was, purifying the City! How fresh the wind, also purifying, dispersing the gusts of warm food-flavoured air that had blown against my face in the morning! What peace in the silence and darkness which had engulfed the streets' tumult! I began to run, my face and body glowing, and my heart, too. There was nothing to fear. If the life in me was good, so was the life outside me. They were the same. I saw all life like small flames dancing out of one fire. The flames flared up and flickered out continuously, yet there were always as many, an infinite number. When they were impure their own smoke soon dulled and extinguished them, like a stove with a choked draught. To flare up and flicker out was their nature, and if the fire from which they came itself burnt out, that was its nature too. 'Oh accept life!' I thought. 'Oh yield to it!'

3

The Kingdoms of the Earth, Spread Out Like a Banquet

Through a Bayswater window I watched an Archdeacon walking briskly home to breakfast after conducting a Communion service. His clothes were velvety black. A silver cross hung on a chain round his neck. His gaitered calves were strong, his movements vigorous, his hair iron-grey. The spring morning was in his nostrils as he stepped along, face pale and serenely furrowed. Dare I intrude on him, fresh from administering the Blessed Sacrament, from dropping wafers in outstretched hands and giving the cup again and again to sip while he earnestly murmured, 'This is my body, this my blood'?

I raced after him. 'Archdeacon,' I said, and paused, not knowing what to say. He looked at me questioningly. 'Archdeacon, is there a God?'

He cleared his throat, glanced for a moment at his watch, and suggested I should walk along with him. 'Now,' he said when we were walking side by side, 'what's your trouble?'

If only I had a trouble! I thought. If only, like the Scientist, I was afraid I might go mad, or drank, or had stolen money or deserted a wife and children! Then, priestly, he would have given me guidance, even though it made him late for breakfast.

'It's only,' I said, ashamed to have interrupted his rapture on so poor a pretext, 'that I'm looking for God.'

His face cleared. 'We'll talk over breakfast,' he said. 'What a lovely morning!' As we walked along he greeted passers-by, and they greeted him back. It was like birds singing in the early morning. The tall house-fronts were bright with sunshine and stood, benign, on either side of us, doorsteps whitened, knockers polished. Smiling, the Archdeacon looked round as though to say, 'You want to see God – look round, my dear fellow, look round. Listen to our footfalls' joyous ring on the stone pavement. See, abundance! – milk, bread, newspapers, all that the heart of Man can desire.'

At his breakfast table *The Times* awaited him, and the *Daily Herald* to give the other side. His wife poured out coffee from a heavy silver pot. She was younger than he was, dark and capable. 'There's a place ready laid,' she said to me. 'Bernard often brings unexpected guests.' She smiled at him indulgently. Letters were piled by his plate. As he sipped his coffee he looked them over; then, as he ate his bacon and egg, turned his attention to me.

'I'll leave you to talk,' his wife said considerately, like a friend at a matrimonial reconciliation.

He assured her there was no need to go. Not a case, he implied, that needed privacy. A woman's presence might even be helpful. 'Tell me about yourself,' he said to me.

'There's nothing to tell,' I said. 'It's merely . . .' After all there was a great deal to tell about myself. Under the stimulus of his interest my life extended. Its colours heightened – flaming sin and black repentance. I had drunk deep of life. I had known love and hate, the full range. 'It's merely that I've been to and fro in the earth, praying at many altars, sleeping with many women . . .'

The Archdeacon winced. His wife did not wince. 'I see what you mean,' he interrupted gently. 'And now?'

I wanted to go on. 'I've tried everything – success and failure, riches and poverty, mortifying the flesh and indulging it . . .'

He cut me short firmly. 'I see, I see.'

'And now I want to be pure of heart and see God.'

He beamed at his wife and she at him.

'I understand exactly,' she said. 'I've been through the same stage myself, haven't I, Bernard?'

He nodded, a little put out that she should bracket herself with me, implying that she and I, a younger generation, had been more adventurous in experimenting with life than he had. When she again got up to go he made no protest.

'Let me tell you,' he said as the door shut behind her, 'of something that happened to me last year. A middle-aged man came to me very much as you have. He told me that in his youth he had defrauded an insurance company. The fraud was not discovered. Then his life was changed. He surrendered himself to God and God told him to confess the fraud. Must he do so? he wanted to know. If he confessed he would have to refund the money he had wrongfully been paid, and that would mean depriving his son of the university education he had saved up to give him; if he did not confess, it would mean disobeying God. Well, we prayed together, and he felt clear that he must confess. It was a terrible test, but he went through with it. After great difficulty he saw the manager of the insurance company, who at first flatly disbelieved him. Then, when he was convinced, he declined to receive back the money. Imagine it! – an insurance company, one of the leading companies in the Kingdom, refusing to be

reimbursed for an authenticated fraud. More than that, the
manager was so impressed that he knelt down then and there
in the man's presence and in his own office, and surrendered
himself to God too, afterwards giving the man a four-
hundred-a-year job. Now the man's rejoined his wife, from
whom he was separated, and his son's starting at Cambridge
next term.'

If only, I thought sadly, I had defrauded an insurance
company, or saved up to give my son a university education.
'Astonishing!' I murmured.

The Archdeacon looked at his watch, and said that he had
only got five minutes more. He suggested that the best way
to spend this five minutes would be in prayer. We knelt
down together among the empty plates and cups, silver
coffee pot now cold, toast-rack with one piece of toast left on
it, fragments of bacon rind in congealed fat. He prayed that
my darkness might be lightened. Eyes tightly closed, voice
earnest, he asked God to take possession of me. When his
prayer was finished he saw me to the front door. As I walked
away I looked back and saw him still in the doorway,

smiling, clothes of velvety black, silver cross on a chain round his neck, and wanted to shout, 'Archdeacon, is there a God?'

Riding along on top of a bus I tried to account for the Archdeacon. How did he come to be? In what distant deeps or skies burnt the fire of his eyes? What forces had planted him in Bayswater, dressed him in velvety black, rounded his calves and danced them along a pavement that spring morning?

In Christ nailed on his cross, dying, and wondering why God had forsaken him, was implicit the Archdeacon breakfasting, reading his letters, collating *The Times* and the *Daily Herald*, and rejoicing that he was unforsaken. That event, matured through centuries, had engendered the Archdeacon. Christ's cross like Aaron's rod, had blossomed, sprouting the little silver cross the Archdeacon wore on a chain round his neck. Christ's despair at being forsaken by God and Man was the origin of the Archdeacon's delight at an insurance company being repaid what it had wrongfully disbursed. If there had been no Calvary there would have been no Archdeacon, no heavy silver coffee pot, no kneeling down, he and I together, to pray that my darkness might be lightened.

Riding along on top of a bus, I saw Calvary – a bedraggled little scene, unmomentous; a few soldiers and sightseers and crying women, a few exultant enemies and a few bewildered friends. Except for Christ's face, it was a paltry scene. This face held by attention. It was unforgettable, so sad and so inscrutable. What was he thinking? I wondered. What was his mood as he slowly, painfully gave up the ghost? Did he regret the lovely earth, or thankfully leave it? Was his heart bitter, or full of pity, or just waiting to be still? He was, I decided, in love with death. Loving life, he could love death, life's culmination, and shake himself free of his mortality tenderly, like a father shaking himself free of his children's embraces when he says goodnight to them. Living had taught him this love of death. It was all there was to be learnt from living.

The Archdeacon's grey eyes shone with a hard lustre; his

pallor was lively and his flesh compact. The Archdeacon was not in love with death. If death had approached him as he sipped his coffee and opened the letters piled by his plate, he would have beaten it determinedly away. Nailed to a cross, his muscles would have been taut, his head erect. Calvary, if he had been crucified there, would have resounded with defiant shouts, and death have seemed to him, not a fulfilment, but a bitter deprivation. How unimaginable a sequence of events from Christ dying to the Archdeacon breakfasting! Who would have supposed that a remote outcome of nailing Christ to a wooden cross would be the Archdeacon striding blithely along after administering Holy Communion? I marvelled at this strange sequence of events – a crucifixion worked on, digested, for two thousand years, and lo! the Archdeacon in velvety black with a silver cross hung on a chain round his neck.

4

Lover of Literature and of Life

I sat in a church on a solid polished pew. The Vicar, thick red curls clustered like bubbles round his neck and ears, climbed into the pulpit and announced a poetry-reading by a famous actress. In the hurly-burly of life, he said, it was good sometimes to withdraw and meditate on God and Eternity. Church services were designed to this end, but he for his part refused to draw any hard and fast distinction between what was secular and sacred. Music or Literature or acting which engendered great thoughts were as much of God as any religious service. He remembered very well meeting a fellow-clergyman, now a Bishop, in St Paul's one evening. 'I've just seen *The Passing of the Third Floor Back*,' the fellow-clergyman had said, 'and felt I had to have a word of prayer.' This had made a great impression on him. Then in the War he had noticed how music, even quite profane music, had helped men to face privation and to turn their thoughts to God. He would never forget how once in a field hospital he had bent over one of the worst cases brought in that day, and the man had whispered, 'Cocksparrow!' (In the trenches he had been 'Cocksparrow' to everyone, and the name had stuck.) 'I don't know any hymns, but I suppose God won't mind "Tipperary".' It was his conviction that of all the anthems of praise which had at different times risen up on high this man's broken rendering of 'Tipperary' was among the most acceptable in God's ears.

His face beamed out, ruddy and amiable, from among the white folds of his surplice. The congregation, a few pewfuls, nodded to his words, reflecting his earnest jocularity in their faces. A man with a trimmed fair beard sitting next to me looked irritated.

'We want Literature,' he whispered, 'not to listen to him.'

'You like Literature?' I whispered back.

'I love Literature,' he answered with shrill intensity.

As the famous actress recited he shaded his pale blue eyes with his hand. She recited a number of Shakespeare's sonnets, explaining before she began that a tedious controversy had led to their beauty and profundity being sometimes over-looked. 'It has been suggested,' she said, 'that these sonnets were inspired by an unnatural passion. I deny it.' Her voice rang tremulously deep through the church. 'Shakespeare's purity is apparent in every line he wrote.' She recited resonantly, loose bosom heaving, chin uplifted, chains and ornaments and bracelets tinkling like cymbals: –

> Full many a glorious morning have I seen
> Flatter the mountain tops with sovereign eye . . .

I forgot Calvary and being in love with death. Morning came, another day, with all its still undisappointed hopes. The day sufficed. I need not look behind it or before. It was enough that there was a day and that I was alive. Seen against the sun-rise, Christ's face was lugubrious. These twilit churches with their candle flames, I thought, and twisted anguished words – what had I to do with them? My life had risen like the morning sun and would go down in the evening, and that was all.

The famous actress went on reciting, her voice a trifle hoarse but not less resonant, her bosom unimpeded in its sway, ornaments clanging more frenziedly: –

> Alas, 'tis true I have gone here and there,
> And made myself a motley to the view,
> Gored mine own thoughts, sold cheap what is most
>   dear . . .

My exaltation died. I had gone here and there, and made myself a motley to the view, thoughts gored and mangled, worked over and over like tired Indian soil. This was what the glorious morning had brought forth.

> Mine appetite I never more will grind . . .

Nevermore, I thought, oh nevermore.

Our love was new and then but in the spring . . .

The recitation was over. The Vicar blessed us and we went away, the man with the trimmed beard walking by my side. His coloured tie was large but neatly tied, and his hands were pink and neat, with a jade ring on the little finger.
'You love Literature,' I said.
He nodded.
'What else do you love?'
He said he loved Life as well as Literature. 'They're the same,' he said. 'Literature and Life are the same.'

'What I mean is,' I said, 'do you love money, women, authority? Do you want to be rich? Do you want to grind your appetite? Do you want to be important?'

I should have liked to confront him suddenly with money, to have held a careless handful of five-pound notes under his nose, or shovelled coins like a bank cashier into his green shirt and seen whether he shivered as their cold touched his warm flesh.

He denied that he loved money.

'You've got some though?' I asked.

'A little.'

'How much?' I insisted.

'Just enough to live on,' he answered petulantly. 'No more than everyone would have if credit were properly distributed.' He went on to explain how easy it would be to distribute credit properly. All that was needed was to apply a Plan. He had written and distributed pamphlets about this Plan, and expounded it at street corners, and inscribed it on a banner and carried the banner to Hyde Park, and shouted it through the Prime Minister's window. 'People will come at last to believe in the Plan,' he said passionately. 'Then there'll be no more poverty.'

'I believe in the Plan,' I said.

It did not enthuse him. He looked at me suspiciously, as though he resented my too easy conversion.

'I'll write a pamphlet for you,' I said.

His face clouded. 'We've got plenty of pamphlets. It's money we want.'

'Swear you don't love money. Swear it!'

'Money's not a thing that can be loved. It's a means of exchange. In itself it's nothing.'

He was quiet and patient. I began to shout. 'Whatever it is, do you love it? – coins, currency notes, cheques, figures in a pass-book. Do they make your heart beat faster? Do they excite?'

'I tell you,' he said, 'it's a means of exchange. It's credit, and can be blown up or deflated like a tyre.'

'Yet you love it,' I insisted. 'You love it as though it had arms to embrace you and flesh to heat your blood.'

'I love Literature,' he said, and began to recite 'Lycidas'. The words dissolved into air as they were spoken. I turned up a side street, leaving him to walk on alone, black hat drooping over his eyes and blond trimmed beard moving as he recited 'Lycidas'.

5

The Albert Hall Rose Up, a Giant

As I waited in the vestibule of the Albert Hall, a youth shouted in my ear, 'It's fun, isn't it?' He was beardless and had no jade ring on his little finger. People pouring into the Albert Hall washed us aside like a strong river. We leant against a wall, breathless.

'Are you changed?' he asked.

'Yes, are you?'

'Oh, I'm changed all right.'

'Grand!' we said together, and shook hands like Swiss mountaineers when they get to the top of a mountain.

'My name's Wimble,' he said.

'And mine's Motley.'

Again we shook hands. Through a swing-door we caught a glimpse of the interior of the Hall – row upon row, tier upon tier of people, so neatly arranged, so orderly, like gymnasts formed into a Union Jack. The organ was playing 'Land of Hope and Glory'.

'They think big, don't they?' Wimble said. 'For the next meeting they've arranged for a hall seating a quarter of a million. They'll fill it too.'

He smiled confidently. There was no limit to the size of hall they could fill. Quarter of a million, half a million, one million – they might get all humanity into a hall and arranged in rows and tiers.

'How were you changed?' Wimble asked.

'It was after listening to a poetry-reading. A man with a trimmed blond beard came up to me and told me he had a Plan. I had no Plan so I accepted his. How were you changed?

He was burning to tell me.

'It was in Manchester,' he said ardently. 'I went with a friend. We'd neither of us thought of anything serious in our

35

lives. Then we heard fellows of our own sort testifying how they'd been changed and felt we ought to testify. It was a bit of an effort, but when I'd got my sins off my chest . . .'

'It wasn't you by chance,' I interrupted, 'who defrauded an insurance company, and then when you tried to pay back the money years afterwards because you were changed they wouldn't take it.'

'No,' he answered regretfully. 'I hadn't done that. Only self-abuse, the usual things. How light my heart was though when I'd spoken them and handed myself over to God!'

We took our places, like swimmers diving into the sea. We were no longer separate. The Albert Hall was a Giant, and we its blood corpuscles. The Giant might stand up and laugh, or roar, or beat his breast in despair, or trample his enemies underfoot. Awed and expectant, we awaited the Giant's mood. Was he angry or jovial or wistful? What was expected of us?

Individuals detached themselves like spray. As we listened we identified ourselves with them. We limped with a retired Admiral to the microphone; we trained racehorses, stroking their warm flanks with fiery tenderness, and growled and swore at our stablemen; then were redeemed, growls dying on our lips and fury in our eyes. Next we were a grey-haired lady from Aberdeen with rimless pince-nez. We quarrelled with our husband and children; we sat icily at meals, spooning up porridge and darting angry looks, until our resentment thawed and we laughed merrily together.

I too longed to detach myself. I wanted to stride on to the platform over shadowy heads, push aside the speakers clustered round the microphone like bees round a flower, and begin: 'I was a reed blown by the wind. I was a voice crying now this, now that. Today a lover, tomorrow a wordling, one role succeeding another, unconnected, soon spent.' Then, beating my breast and firing my eyes, 'Oh the weariness of pleasure's restless pursuit! Oh the emptiness of success and the bitterness of failure! Oh expense of spirit in a waste of shame!' Grave and earnest, words deliberately spoken, 'I cancel it all. I surrender myself to God's guidance. I ask you to do the same.'

Would they not leap from their places, each shouting, 'I will, I will' – one 'I will, I will!' the Giant's? Should I not have them then at my mercy, the Giant at my mercy, to be bidden, as I chose, weep, laugh, rise up mightily, lie down lamb-like? Was it so difficult, concentrating all those neatly arranged rows and tiers of voices into my single voice, all those separate beings into my being? Was God at last revealed? – Eternity adding day to day, Infinity adding one to one, God adding individual to individual, then melting them and running them molten into one another until their

37

hearts were one heart – mine, and their voices one voice – mine, and lo! God – myself.

Now a harsh, insistent voice forced us to leave our harmonious breakfast-table in Aberdeen and get up in the grey dawn, yawning and rubbing our eyes, to clatter through black empty streets and past pale yellow lights, and then dive down into the dark earth. Hair black and close-cropped, cheeks lean, eyes near together, we dwelt lovingly on our depravity – lying, stealing, cheating, gambling, drinking, whoring. We chanted our litany of sin, eyes glowing, flesh tingling. Thus we were, and thus; this we did, and this, parading our sins as an auctioneer parades his lots – 'Here's a fine piece of adultery with deceit to match; here a miscellaneous collection of thieving, lying, drunkenness.' The Albert Hall grew fetid. Its air was thick and heavy, tiers and rows like shelves in an attic piled with decaying fruit. I got up and went away.

Outside the Albert Hall I continued to chant – 'I lied, I stole . . .' A consciousness of sin, deep sin, dwelt with me. I smelt sin like bodies in the dressing-room of a swimming-bath on a hot day, and saw souls being unwrapped like feet after a sweltering walk. Evil blistered to the surface in sores and boils exposed by wailing Oriental beggars, and the shapes of people hurrying past were sinister shadows flitting about a swamp.

A little company was gathered round a harmonium and singing a hymn. I sang with them. An elderly man with a grey straggling moustache said when the hymn was over, 'God is love,' and then, 'The Kingdom of Heaven is within.'

I touched his arm. 'It's true, but still I'm afraid.'

He looked at me mildly. 'If God is love whatever is false must perish and only what is true live; and if the Kingdom of Heaven is within, and what comes out of a man defiles him and not what goes in, no harm can befall the pure in heart.'

'You fear nothing, then?'

'Only my sinful heart.'

'That's much.'

'It would be much except for God's mercy.'

'How to be pure of heart?' I groaned, still chanting my litany of sin: 'I hated, I coveted, I deceived . . .'

'He maketh His sun to rise on the Evil and on the Good, and sendeth rain on the Just and on the Unjust,' the man with the grey straggling moustache said, and started another hymn.

The evening was mild and fragrant, the trees newly green. People lingered in Hyde Park, enjoying the spring twilight, strolling over the grass and clinging together in twos and little groups, not arranged in rows and tiers, not digits in an immense total; children belonging to one family; all different, all separate, each the centre of a universe, yet all connected, the old and the young, lovers and elderly married couples, children and aged spinsters with little dogs on leads; connected, I thought, because a part of the same creation, infused with the same spirit, born of Eternity and alive in Time and soon to die.

'Airing ourselves in Hyde Park on a spring evening,' I thought; 'holding an arm or a hand or a dog's lead, looking up at the sky or down at the grass or in one another's eyes, hoping and planning and reckoning up our money, drawing apart or clasping together, waiting for night to come and then for morning to break and then for night to come again, all warmed by the same sun, all watered by the same rain, all inflamed by the same passions, all having the same imperfections and the same obscure longings – we may grow awry, yet we seed and each seed begins again: calamities may overtake us and lay us waste, yet the life that is in us goes on, as parched fields some time recover their green; we may ourselves destroy our own fertility, and make a wilderness of our own habitations, and seek darkness and horror, yet there must still be June evenings and people strolling over the new grass, solitary or clinging together in twos or little groups.'

6

Flavell, by the Serpentine

By the Serpentine five ungainly ladies and Flavell were sitting on a bench and taking in the sun. They took in the sun thirstily through opened mouths, leaning back their heads and closing their eyes. I sat down beside Flavell, leant back my head, closed my eyes, and opened my mouth.

'It's the best way of spending time,' Flavell said. The sun had burnt two angry spots on his pale cheeks, and made his eyes bloodshot. 'Especially in a town. Activity all round makes indolence the more delightful.'

What activity inside him! – thoughts hurrying along like men along Cheapside, hopes anxiously counted over like change; mind tapping, tapping, like a typewriter. 'One may not,' I thought, 'always agree with Mr Flavell; he may not always be comprehensible, but he is a force to be reckoned with.'

'What are you writing now?' I asked.

He turned his eyes anxiously away from the sun to look at me, as though he suspected I had some special reason for asking what he was writing.

'Why?' he asked nervously.

'I only wondered.'

'I'm writing a novel,' he said, 'about a working-class family.'

In the evening, having lain fallow all day by the Serpentine, he would sit in his room over a dry-cleaner's in Marchmont Street, and drink tea and smoke cigarettes and work at his novel about a working-class family. The bit he did yesterday about Amyas not being able to wait for Enid until he had taken off his pit clothes, and having her on the stone kitchen floor while the bath she had prepared for him got cold – needed re-touching. It was not quite right. As he took in the sun through his opened mouth Flavell went over the scene.

'When I was in Alexandria,' Flavell said, 'I used to lie all day on the beach, and watch Greek boys going in and out of the sea; and then in the evenings we used to carouse naked on the roof of an Egyptian millionaire's house, and eat raw onions, and drink thick Cyprus wine. I've never felt so in tune with the universe as then.'

I saw him, breath reeking of onions, somnolent with thick Cyprus wine, in tune with the universe.

'Are you in tune with the universe now?' I asked.

He said he was not, or at best partially. There was not enough sun by the Serpentine for him to be wholly in tune with the universe. He had to wear too many clothes. The struggle to live was too overpowering. It obtruded on his peace as he sat by the Serpentine taking in the sun through his opened mouth.

'That's what my novel's about,' he said eagerly, sun forgotten, immense beaked nose a shadow across his face – 'the struggle to live.'

'This remarkable novel,' I read on the flap of a dust-cover, 'traces the fortunes of a working-class family through three generations. It movingly shows how privation and in-security break the spirit of the old people, until Enid, a granddaughter who has managed in spite of great difficulties to get an education, shows them all that salvation lies in revolt. Woven into the story is the love of Amyas Dudding for Enid. She turns from him because he does not share her cultural background, but returns to him at last – to work for his parliamentary candidature.'

One of the five ungainly ladies coughed and glanced down at her *Daily Express*.

'Flavell, are you ambitious?' I asked. 'Do you see in a vision sometimes your name printed in large letters? Do you hope that people will nudge one another when you pass by and whisper, "That's Flavell!" Does a longing to be im-portant eat at your heart – even in the sun, even on the beach at Alexandria, or carousing on raw onions and thick Cyprus wine on the roof of an Egyptian millionaire's house?'

He denied that he was ambitious – fingernails gnawed

away and raw flesh showing above them. 'If I'd been am-
bitious,' he said, 'I shouldn't have refused to go into the
Civil Service when I was top in all England in the Civil
Service Examination. Grayson, who was below me, is
Finance Minister in Kenya; Thoroughgood, whom I beat by
three marks, is an important Treasury official, and knighted
– Sir Francis Thoroughgood.'

He laughed bitterly, and, looking up petulantly, besought
the sun to consume his pride at having been top in all
England in the Civil Service Examination. He remembered
the hours and hours he had spent reading, making notes,
attending lectures, lying in bed with his mind running over
questions he might have to answer, and thought of Grayson's
pension and Thoroughgood's knighthood, and of how he had
just missed getting a fellowship at Cambridge, and of his
room above a dry-cleaner's in Marchmont Street with sheets
of paper littered on the table, and cups with dregs of tea in
them, and glasses with dregs of beer, and a half-eaten slice of
bread and butter that had lain three days on his mantel-

piece, and how he was behind with his novel about a working-class family. Clouds blew up, and the seven of us sitting on a bench by the Serpentine were suddenly cold and forlorn. No sun came into our opened mouths or warmed our upturned faces. We shivered and got up.

Flavell took me to a bar. 'I love bars,' he said. 'People are human in bars. I've heard wonderful things said in bars.' The bar we went into had just opened. Flavell sidled up to a Negro, whispering, 'How lovely he is! I'd love to see him dive, like a dark leaf falling gently into a river on a still autumn day.'

The Negro told us that his name was Fernandez, and that he played in a dance orchestra, and that his wife had discarded him, preferring a lodger named Prothero. She had, he complained, locked him out of his own house, and he had had to take a room near by. As he spoke of this his voice broke, and he suddenly began to cry, opening his mouth wide and howling. Flavell looked across at me significantly and whispered, 'How touching! And how real!' He listened

delightedly to the Negro's howls, and put his arm round his heaving shoulders, and paid for a drink for him, paying this cash tribute to his muscles and broad back and easy tears.

I saw Mrs Fernandez, a blonde untidy woman with false teeth and a pink face, and Prothero making his way home to her late at night across Hyde Park, bald pate glowing, exuberant, and reeling a little, the lights of passing motor cars luxuriant, like a countryside after rain; at last falling with a groan into Mrs Fernandez's arms while Fernandez, dress-shirted, blew through a trombone, crooning, grinning, shouting, grimacing, urging tired dancers to renewed efforts.

Flavell clung to the Negro when the three of us walked away from the bar together. It was a gesture of defiance, like his novel about a working-class family. He hoped to steal strength from the Negro to enliven Enid and Amyas, as he had hoped to steal strength from the sun to forget his triumph in being first in all England in the Civil Service Examination. He clung to the Negro's arm and held mine loosely. There were heavy clouds in the sky, and no sun to be taken in by the Serpentine. It was an oppressive dull afternoon. 'Lend me a pound,' the Negro said suddenly to Flavell.

Sidelong, I watched Flavell's face stiffen. His mouth tightened, his eyes sheltered fearfully behind his large nose. He drew away from the Negro without letting go his arm, and said he had only a few shillings.

'You lend me a pound,' the Negro repeated, his voice leaden as the sky.

Flavell said it might be possible to get to his bank in time to cash a cheque. He walked miserably towards his bank so dejected now, and still clinging to the Negro's arm and loosely holding mine. At the bank he detached himself, and went alone to the counter, and there wrote a cheque. What a concentration of purpose in him as he wrote it! What strength! Mr Flavell was indeed a force to be reckoned with.

The counter was thronged with reverent faces. Pieces of paper were passed across it, voices and light subdued, swing-doors silently opening and shutting. Restless doubt had not entered here. This was a citadel of faith, a sanctuary. 'It is good for us to be here,' I whispered to the Negro. 'Let us build here three tabernacles.' He did not hear me. He was watching Flavell as the cashier handed him five pound notes – the cashier priestly in vestments of black, administering the Blessed Elements, paper and silver, to his flock and sending them away satisfied; as he counted over piles of pound notes occasionally moistening his forefinger; shovelling coins on to a scale-pan. His face grey and impassive, the cashier shed peace on all around him. Even on Flavell, who forgot Thoroughgood's knighthood and Grayson's pension, left his fingernails ungnawed, dismissed all concern about Amyas and Enid from his mind, as he waited for his five pound notes, received them, counted them over, reluctantly detached one and handed it to the Negro, and put the other four away in his hip-pocket. Like worshippers in a church waiting a few moments after the service is finished before getting up to go, Flavell waited a few moments, brow serene, eyelids lowered, after he had put away his four pound notes before leaving the bank. Then without taking the Negro's arm again he said that he must go and work, and the Negro said that he must go to a rehearsal, and I was left alone.

7

Lust, Along the Euston Road

For company I had only Lust. Lust clung to my back, and I bent under the weight; Lust was fire in my veins, and an insistent voice in my ears; Lust twisted itself into my thoughts and harried my heart, and distorted my vision. Along the Euston Road I saw immense blossoms, swollen and coloured and scentless, and heavy trees whose branches clanged metallically in the wind. The air was warm and full of smiles and sombre faces bearing them; and red buses glided by, and fragments of talk, and shrill laughter. I saw Lust everywhere – on hoardings, in clothes, in shop windows, rumbling over bridges, huddled under archways, cast off like a garment, put on like a garment, painted like a clown's face, still like a skull, warm as a fever and cold as death.

What was there, I thought, more profitable than Lust? If in the vastness of London there were doorways, street names, bus routes, that glowed for me with an inward richness, it was because I associated them with Lust. Would the Archdeacon's front door seem fiery because I had prayed with him behind it? Yet if, instead of praying with him, I had passed my hand lightly, quickly, over his parlourmaid, finding a furtive opportunity – dare I then pass the front door at all? Dare I even think of it, burnt into my being like stigmata, unforgettable? If, looking back, a space of time stood out like green grass in a desert, a poignant hour or day or even several days, it was because of Lust. Lust made Time gleam and tremble, as sunlight did dust floating in air. It revealed Time's texture. If, instead of walking aimlessly along the Euston Road, I had been bent on Lust's business, what vigour and what purpose in my step! What rich colours and radiant faces and eternal delight!

How on a warm afternoon in the Euston Road was satisfaction to be obtained? I scrutinized each passing face.

Leering and grimacing, I offered my Lust with money to sweeten it. I peddled my Lust along the Euston Road, but no one wanted it. It was a dead weight on my heart, a burden to be endured. I was like a commercial traveller wearily going from door to door with an unwanted commodity. In a basement restaurant I rested, mechanically offering my Lust to the waitress, who turned away. All day long Lust washed round her, like hot air or steam. It made her tired and flaccid. The rouge dripped from her lips and the powder congealed in little gobbets on her cheeks, Lust so tired her. A Russian orchestra in green shirts with high collars played, blowing and twanging and crooning their Lust, the conductor frenzied in his efforts to get the last particle of Lust out of them. They must give their Lust like a blood-donor his blood to enliven the dying. It was a Lust-transfusion, and revived ebbing appetites. I listened, alternately drying my mouth with tobacco smoke and moistening it with tea.

Lust ran through my life like a flaming thread. It was like a pageant, scene after scene with intervening twilight – clasped in passionate virginity on a horsehair sofa under the shadow of a bamboo flower-pot stand and tall black piano littered with 'There are Fairies at the Bottom of Our Garden', 'Tread Softly, Tread Softly, because you tread on my Dreams', 'Less than the Dust'; crouching with a horsehair dressing-gown pricking my bare skin and starting at every sound, and then sitting bare-headed with the rain gently falling, at peace, at peace for a moment; on all fours like a pig, lean shanks under shirt and plump thighs under chemise, prancing and capering on a thick horsehair carpet with four glowing bars, mathematical – scene after scene.

8

Margaretta Barfoot, on her Divan

I went to see Margaretta Barfoot about doing something for German-Jewish refugees. 'Something ought to be done,' she said. 'I quite see that. I've started this little publication.'

She handed me a copy. It was called *Freedom*, and I turned over the pages as I lolled among coloured cushions in front of a gas fire.

'Perhaps it'll do some good,' she went on.

'Perhaps it will,' I agreed.

She was beside me among the coloured cushions. They were like coloured waves buoying us up, washing us this way and that. Over their crests I caught occasional glimpses of her small eyes and fringe of blonde hair and small regular teeth.

'We're free, aren't we?' I said. 'It's wonderful to be free. No pang of fear comes to either of us when I take you in my arms so, does it? Words like "sin" and "adultery" have lost their sting for us, haven't they? We'll quench our Lust together, won't we? and then be at ease – oh, lovely ease! Oh peace after Lust's torment!'

Lust glowed in my eyes and in hers. Our eyes glowed like electric bulbs, then went out leaving darkness.

'What are you doing nowadays?' she asked.

'Nothing.'

She laughed. 'Nothing! How amusing. I'm sure you're doing something really. I'm writing a book.'

'About a working-class family?'

'Not exactly,' she answered doubtfully. We were adjusting our clothes while we talked.

She began to tell me the plot of her book. 'It's about a woman who's married to a famous scientist. She admires and respects him, but is haunted by a feeling that their relationship is somehow inadequate. There's no passion in it, she

49

feels, and this worries her. Then she meets one of her husband's assistants, also a clever scientist but a failure, and very ugly, whereas her husband, of course, is good-looking . . .'

Her voice droned on, her little eyes slightly bloodshot now, as Flavell's were from the sun and her little regular teeth venomous like a ferret's.

'. . . Most of the action takes place while she's under an anaesthetic having a baby which may be her husband's and may be his assistant's. She doesn't know and comes to see that it doesn't matter. It matters to her emotionally, but it doesn't matter socially. That's the point. It just doesn't matter socially one way or the other.'

The reference to having a baby caught my wandering attention. 'Talking of having babies,' I began.

Her loose mouth suddenly stiffened, like Flavell's when the Negro asked for a pound, or when he counted over the five pound notes the cashier gave him. 'That's all right,' she

interrupted. A little clip made of gold had been fastened on to her womb's aperture to close it.

Secure in the knowledge of this little golden clip, I became brave. 'I'd like you to have a child by me. It would be marvellous. Do have one. Why not?'

She shook her head, mouth still firm, and only relaxing, splaying out, as she went on with her account of the novel she was writing.

'It's been delightful,' I said, getting up to go and kissing her brow. 'It'll remain a delightful memory. Whenever I think of this room, this street, the bus that brought me here, I'll get a pang of excitement. Every time I turn over the pages of a telephone directory I'll think of how I might ring you up and spend another afternoon with you among these coloured cushions. We've been happy together. That's the strongest of bonds – to have been happy with someone. And nothing can destroy our happiness. It's enriched and purified us, and hurt no one. It's added to the store of happiness in the world . . .' I wanted to get away and so choked back the flow of words rising like groans from my heavy heart. 'You really must do that novel. It sounds most promising. I'll get it to review and see that it gets plenty of reviews. Let me know in good time about the date of publication. I should like to become a subscriber to *Freedom*. I'll give you a year's subscription now if you like. No, I'll post it to you if you don't mind. I'll post you a cheque this evening without fail. As you say, something ought to be done about the German-Jewish refugees. Something ought to be done . . .' I ejected words as a slug ejects slime, to ease my passage away.

'That's Ernst,' she said, showing me an enlarged snapshot of a German-Jew wearing bathing slips and drinking tea by Lake Maggiore. 'He's rather lovely, isn't he?'

I agreed that he was rather lovely with his black smooth hair and dark eyes and soft tanned limbs. 'I'd like you to meet Flavell some time,' I said. 'He's rather lovely, too.'

Over Hampstead Heath lovers were crouching, immobile in one another's arms, still and silent. I eyed these lovers curiously, twined together under trees or on wooden seats or wherever there was shadow. Lust still burnt and groaned in me; an unsteady flame, reflected and magnified in the ponderous glow London threw into the sky; echoed in the distant rumble of traffic. How many little flames of Lust burning in how many breasts made up that glow! How many groans in how many breasts made up that distant rumble!

A figure detached itself from the trees, unsteady, breath acrid and hot in the cool evening air, bare pate glowing and face glowing, occasionally straining like stew trying to boil over, and then subsiding.

'It's wonderful,' he said. 'I don't know why all London isn't here. A tree to sit under when it's over and the stars to look at, and no talk, old boy, no talk. Oh, wonderful! I gave her five shillings and she was delighted. She used to be at the Elephant and Castle, but says she prefers it here, and by Jove so do I.'

'I didn't pay five shillings,' I said, 'but there was talk.'

'Not pay five shillings?' He looked at me wonderingly.

'What did you pay?'

'A little Lust,' I said. 'No more.'

'A little Lust,' he repeated after me. 'No more.'

We walked along together. Suddenly I recognized him. 'I know,' I said, 'you're Prothero.'

'If you like,' he said.

'And you're on your way to Mrs Fernandez. She's waiting for you. How can you go to her now, after spending your five shillings?'

'I'll go to her no matter what I've spent. I'll always go to her.' He began to sob on my shoulder. 'I love her, I love her.' The sobbing made him boil over. After he had turned aside to be sick he said, 'I'm so miserable.'

I patted his shoulder. 'There there. We're all in the same boat whatever we pay, money or Lust or hope. Think of Tolstoy in his wife's arms beating his breast and tearing at his beard and shouting, "Woe, woe!" Think of Dickens lustfully pacing London streets, up and down, up and down, and of Wordsworth turning away in horror from a naked man and woman made of stone, and savagely muttering, "It's the Devil!" and of Shakespeare's "There's hell, there's darkness, there's the sulphurous pit, burning, scalding, stench, consumption," and of Samuel Butler walking to his mistress every Wednesday afternoon with a gold coin clutched in one hand and a sponge-bag in the other, and of me among Margaretta Barfoot's coloured cushions and of you underneath a tree. Look! Lust glowing in the sky, flavouring the air, springing from the earth, rotting back into the earth.'

From the top of Parliament Hill we looked down on London. It was spread beneath us, like a lake with stars reflected in it.

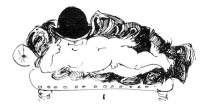

9

I Dreamed that I Lay Dying

That night I dreamed that I lay dying in Geneva. My bed
was in a large darkened room. There were plush curtains
drawn to, and a thick dusty carpet. The furniture was heavy
and old, with cigarette boxes and newspapers and ash trays
and books in their dust-covers scattered about. It was a mild
September day. I knew that outside the sun was shining, and
that people would be sitting in cafés by the Lake, and reading
newspapers, and watching steamers come and go. In the
darkened room a fire was burning. I felt a great weakness in
myself. All my energies seemed to be ebbing away, and I
resented this, and tried to prevent it, raising myself and then
falling back helplessly. My hair was white and thin, and I had
a white trimmed moustache. When I looked at my hands I
saw that they were shrivelled and frail, with the veins in
them swollen.

Mariette was sitting beside me. She had red hair and
rouged lips and cheeks, and a black tight dress that irritated
me because it had been put down to my account and the bill
kept coming in. As she waited for me to die she embroidered
a green swallow on a salmon-pink silk chemise she had
made. Her body was pungent, like an over-ripe fruit.

'Read me the newspaper,' I said petulantly.

No newspaper had come that day, she indicated, pouting
her lips and spreading out her hands.

'Why?' I asked.

She rubbed the ball of her thumb against her forefinger.
Money – she wanted money. How hard and cruel she looked
as she rubbed the ball of her thumb against her forefinger!
I shook my head. She fetched my cheque-book and fountain-
pen and put them on the small table beside my bed, then
went on with her embroidering.

'I can't write a cheque,' I moaned, and took the fountain-
pen and the cheque-book and in a faltering hand wrote a

cheque for twenty Swiss francs. Mariette snatched it eagerly, looked at the amount, and sprayed me with spittle as she blew contemptuously through her mouth. While she went to cash the cheque and buy a newspaper I looked at the ceiling, and thought: 'Death should be quiet, a quiet grateful loosening of the senses' grip: –

I have lived long enough: my way of life
Is fallen into the sear, the yellow leaf.

There should be children awaiting a last blessing and loving hands to close my eyes for the last time.' Ghosts gathered round of all the bodies I'd belaboured, echoes of all the love I'd sworn to. My heart was dry and parched, and full of the ashes of spent Lust. My heart was cold, and dreaded the chill creeping over my body. The only warmth left was my body's, and that was fading, and I had no strength left to revive it.

Mariette read aloud to me from the *Journal de Genève*. There had been a meeting of the League of Nations; speeches had been made and a resolution passed. I felt a pang of anxiety. Things were happening and I did not know. Events had left me behind. I ought perhaps to send a telegram. Boncour would have arranged with Titulescu . . . My mind collapsed. Arranged what? I did not know. Boncour and Titulescu might be out of office, or dead, for all I knew. 'The telephone,' I whispered, and began to cry for helplessness, and because I knew I should never more type urgent words (urgent today, and tomorrow as uncertain as Boncour and Titulescu), or shout them into a telephone; never more sit in warm cafés overflowing with conversation, or expectantly unfold a newspaper, or wait in cold corridors for a word to be spoken or a hastily typed communiqué to be put in my hands.

Mariette saw me crying, and said: '*Pauvre petit*,' and put a flat cigarette between my lips. As she held a lighted match to it I sucked in scented smoke, then let the cigarette fall on to the coverlet. '*Pauvre petit*,' Mariette said again, and bent over me. I felt her ripe breath on my face, and saw her lips, swollen and fiery, approaching mine that were shrivelled, bloodless.

'*Tu m'aimes, Mariette?*' I gasped.

'*Oui, mon petit, je t'aime bien.*'

Her lips approached like a consuming flame. They bore down on me scorching up what remained of my life. I struggled, choking, with darkness breaking over me in wave after wave.

10

Friend, in Trafalgar Square

Lolling by a lion in Trafalgar Square I envied each passer-by his purpose. How blessed, I thought, to be in a hurry, to have some urgent appointment to keep, to be looking anxiously for clocks hoping they had stayed still instead of dreading to see them because their hands moved so sluggishly. How blessed, I thought, to be a bus-driver, so many times to and from Camden Town, and then home, in the winter to sit over a fire, in the summer to take a stroll through Regent's Park; how blessed to be a tobacconist, serving packets of cigarettes and tobacco, then counting the day's takings, and locking up his shop in the dusk.

Time drifted by slowly like a slow river and I was an idler staring down at it from a bridge. By the steps of St Martin's-in-the-Fields a man wound up little clockwork men and pigs, and danced them on the pavement. They danced merrily and then suddenly stopped as though paralysed, feet poised for a step that was never completed. I watched Friend pick his way among these clockwork men and pigs, his movements more stately than theirs, overshadowing them. A blond silky moustache waved round his full loose mouth. His suit was dark, and he carried a black leather satchel and a rolled umbrella.

'Friend!' I shouted. 'Friend!'

His manner when he recognized me was non-committal. There might, he seemed to be saying to himself, be some reason at present unknown to him for treating me with consideration. I might, for instance, have inherited a legacy, or been appointed to an important post; or I might have written a book that was going to attract attention. Until he knew just how things were with me it was unwise to define our relations.

'What are you doing now?' he asked.

'Nothing.'

'Nothing!' He was shocked and turned away. Nothing should come of nothing.

'Nothing except look for God,' I added.

He paused irresolute. There were possibilities in looking for God. Successful books had been written about looking for God. Unknown preachers passionately intent on that search had become prominent and important. Men like Wesley and Booth would have been useful contacts in their later years.

'If I can be of any help,' he began.

'You can,' I interrupted eagerly. 'Tell me what you want. Tell me what drives you along, why you got up this morning, combed your moustache, cleaned your teeth, shaved; what it is that propels you now across Trafalgar Square, down Whitehall; whence comes your back's sinuousness, your hands' persuasive movements, your voice's softness. Tell me, Friend, what drives you along.'

'If I can be of any help,' he repeated, 'I'm at your service. At the moment – it's not for publication – I'm making all the arrangements in connection with an important foreign personage's forthcoming visit to London. He wants to meet prominent people, and of course is anxious to get some notice in the Press – little incidental paragraphs, you understand, arising naturally out of some topic which happens to be in the news. He's very keen on sanitation, for instance, and has spent a lot of money improving the sanitation in his State. When sanitation gets into the news – there's some conference of sanitary experts on we'll say – it would be easy to get little paragraphs published here and there to the effect that the most up-to-date system of sanitation has been installed in such a State, and that incidentally the head of this State will shortly be visiting London. You get the idea? I'd give you facts and figures of course. You must meet him when he's here. He's very rich. Money's no object with him.' He smiled. 'No object at all. I'm arranging a tea party in his honour, if possible at the House of Lords. In fact I'm on my way to see about it now. I'll see you get an invitation.'

59

'Thank you,' I said humbly. 'That'll be a great help.'

I saw Friend at the tea party at the House of Lords, picking his way among the guests, unostentatious, here smiling, there nodding, there resting his hand for a moment on an arm. How precisely he judged the greeting due! In how masterly a way he carried out his duties! He was like the conductor of a large orchestra, stirring up sound with a twist of his wrist, damping it down with another – now obsequious himself, now evoking obsequiousness; now making deferential introductions, now being deferentially introduced. 'Is it money, Friend?' I pleaded, 'or honours? or the companionship of the Great? Let me into the secret of your purpose. I have no purpose.'

A long black car stopped near us; a voice shouted, 'Friend!' Without answering me he turned away, and the car gathered him up as the whirlwind gathered up Elijah, and I was left lonely by my lion watching Time drift by like a slow river, and wondering still what propelled Friend, whence came his persistence, his industry, the dry hard light in his eyes. As I wondered he became magnified. The lions in Trafalgar Square grew blond silky moustaches, and the traffic moved like guests at a House of Lords tea party, and clocks chimed persuasively, and each passing face met mine appraisingly. Friend was everywhere; Friend was every-thing. There was no escaping Friend or forgetting him. I met him at every turn; his voice whispered in my ear when I closed my eyes at night and greeted me when I opened them in the morning. Though I fled to a remote desert or lived in a walled prison, there was always Friend. 'You're the World, Friend,' I shouted against the traffic's roar. 'You're the Kingdoms of the Earth – Friend OBE, Baron Friend, Earl Friend, Comrade Friend, Commissar Friend, Leader Friend, the Right Honourable Friend, the Right Reverend Friend, President Friend, everlasting, all powerful, omnipresent Friend . . .' I shook my fist in the air. The lions with their blond silky moustaches looked down at me serenely, clocks chimed complacently, motor cars made their way – twisting, turning, stopping, starting, hooting, darting, made their

way round Trafalgar Square like guests at a crowded tea party. My fingers clutched Friend's throat. He was Apollyon and I wrestled with him, falling at his feet and preparing to meet my end.

Then I remembered I had still a weapon. Though my strength would not prevail against Friend's, though I was one against his host, though I was poor and without resources when he had all the earth's riches, still I might denounce him. I saw myself as a slim David armed with a sling going out to fight a Goliath with a blond silky moustache and black suit and satchel and rolled umbrella. Racing through the streets I reached a winding wooden stairway, climbed it, dark and creaking, to the top, and burst into Wilberforce's office.

Wilberforce was seated at his desk, papers littered about it, a sheet of paper fastened in his typewriter. Hair fell disorderly like darkness about his face, and through it restless eyes peered. 'We go to Press today. You've come at a bad time,' he said. 'I've only got an hour to finish this leader.'

'What's it on?' I asked.

'War.' He rubbed his hands together. His eyes shone through his dark hair like lighted windows in a dark forest. 'It's on War. I point out that if the Government pursues its present policy there must be War, that War will destroy civilization, that its inevitable consequence will be revolutions everywhere, but that still at this eleventh hour . . .'

'Let me write your leader,' I interrupted. 'I've got a leader I want to write. I want to write a leader about Friend. I want to demolish him, roll him in the mud, trample him underfoot.'

'It's absurd,' Wilberforce said irritably. 'You're wasting my time. Why, I don't even know who Friend is.'

'He's the World,' I shouted. 'He's Society. He's your enemy and mine. He's the Established Social Order. Let me show that the strands of his silky moustache bind more securely than the strongest manacles, that his soul is a little underground cell in which prisoners languish, that his black suit and satchel and rolled umbrella are darkness hiding the sun. I'd call the leader "*A La Lanterne – Friend!*" '

'You couldn't use his name anyway,' Wilberforce said, looking down at his typewriter keyboard. 'That would be far too dangerous. You'd have to use a fictitious name and make him a fictitious character. The moustache would have to go if it's characteristic, which I assume it is; and it would be safer to put him in a light suit. In fact, why not make him a foreigner, a German say; then you'd be absolutely safe. There may be a miscellany article in it. I don't know. You'd have to submit it, and I'd have to think the whole matter over carefully.'

'Just a little leader,' I pleaded, 'a paragraph after all the others, no more than a sentence or two.'

'The leaderettes are all set,' Wilberforce said, turning them over. 'Spain, road-deaths, birth-control, India, the BBC, the Far East. I couldn't possibly fit in another. Besides' – angrily – 'I tell you you can't write leaders about an individual you happen to dislike and that no one else has heard of. Why, he might be one of our readers himself!'

'He is,' I said eagerly. 'Of course he is one of your readers. That's why I want to write a leader on him.'

Wilberforce began to stab at his typewriter, face contorting, eyes twitching. 'You can have a book to review if you like,' he said, typing, little hammers savagely rising and falling. 'Ask Miss Annerley for a book. Wait a minute' – jumping up – 'what are you interested in?'

I said I was interested in Lust and in Money and in God.

'I've seen a book lying about that might be suitable.' He went into the next room, reappeared with a book and gave it to me. 'Short notice if worth it. Wait for me if you like. We'll have a talk.'

Back at his typewriter, flashing eyes and floating hair, little hammers so furiously rising and falling that they collided, pipe anxiously sucked, a slight froth collecting at the corners of his mouth and then trickling along the pipe-stem – back at his typewriter he was exalted. I looked over his shoulder and read: –

The armaments race in which this country is now making the pace can have only one end – a disastrous War. British policy, unhappily, is designed, not to check but rather to encourage Fascist aggression, and so to hasten . . .

He looked up, tormented. 'To hasten what? To hasten what?'
'An outbreak of War,' I suggested.
'I've used "War" in the last sentence.'
'A European conflagration.'
He nodded and resumed his typing.

. . . hasten a European conflagration. We for our part take the view . . .'

Now he was easy. Now he touched the keyboard confidently, like a pianist playing a familiar tune. His brow cleared, his mouth steadied, the creases gathered round his eyes lost their tension. He knew what view they for their part took. No hesitating now, no doubts; words flowed from his mind into the tips of his fingers and his fingers danced them out joyously, like the little clockwork men and pigs dancing on the pavement outside St Martin's- in-the-Fields. He knew, oh he knew. He tapped steadily, mechanically, familiarly. Awed, I tiptoed into the next room and sat with Miss Annerley waiting for him to finish.

Behind Miss Annerley there were shelves of new books reaching to the ceiling. They towered above her, rows of books, large and small, fiction and non-fiction, prose and verse, Travel, Philosophy, Criticism, Sport, Politics, Economics, Religion.

'Miss Annerley,' I said, agitated, 'it looks as though there's going to be War, unless at this eleventh hour . . .' I faltered. 'At this eleventh hour . . . unless . . .'

She trembled, a short powdery woman with grey hair and a loose green dress. 'Unless what?' she asked anxiously.

'You'll see in Wilberforce's leader when it comes,' I said.

She made tea on a gas ring and opened a packet of three digestive biscuits.

'I dread War more than ever just now,' Miss Annerley said, 'because . . . because I'm pregnant.'

I showed no surprise. Miss Annerley was pregnant. In Miss Annerley's womb a child was taking shape, soon to be born.

'I don't know why I'm telling you this,' she went on tumultuously. 'I haven't told anyone else, except of course the father.'

'The father is pleased?' I asked gravely.

'Oh yes, he's pleased. We're both pleased. Ever since it started I've had such a sense of the richness of life, the fertility of life. Two years ago I had an abortion in Paris, but this is my first real pregnancy.'

We leant side by side out of the little grimy window, high up, and looking over a great expanse of untidy roofs and church spires and the dome of St Paul's, all misted over with smoke. Miss Annerley's cheek was close to mine. I turned and kissed her, plunging my tongue into her mouth still gritty with digestive biscuit.

'No,' she said. 'Please. I don't feel like it just now. You understand . . .'

We returned to the shelves of books. I looked at one or two. Through the partition we could hear Wilberforce typing. He was working to a climax. 'Surely,' I thought, 'this must be the last triumphant conclusion,' but he went on. It was like waiting for an orchestra to finish. At last Wilberforce stopped. I found him drooping over his typewriter. 'Is it War?' I asked anxiously. For answer he handed me his leader, some of it already in proof, little damp pieces of proof. I read it through.

'War, I'm afraid.'

He nodded, eyes shining. 'Good, isn't it? Well written. I must say I think it's rather good.'

'Poor Miss Annerley!' I said. 'Woe unto them that are with child and to them that give suck in those days.'

11

Children of Men

The three of us, Wilberforce, Miss Annerley, and I, walked to Wilberforce's constituency. Wilberforce made the pace. He strode along, hatless, with springing steps. I held Miss Annerley's hand tightly in mine, and she clung to Wilberforce's arm. The streets we walked through got meaner. Wilberforce denounced them. 'It makes me feel ashamed,' he said, 'ashamed not to be hungry and tired and ill-housed. I feel I ought to identify myself with these people. I feel I belong to them. I do what I can, but it's not enough.' He looked anxiously at the hoardings, and was at last rewarded by seeing one of his election posters: 'Vote for Wilberforce and Peace.' We paused in front of it, and I took off my hat and shouted, 'Vote for Wilberforce!' One or two passers-by looked up curiously – men going home from work, women with bags going home from shopping, children playing in the twilight, loiterers waiting for night to come and let them lie down and wait for another day to come.

'Don't you care?' Wilberforce shouted. Their indifference made him indignant. He hated them as they turned indifferently away, hurrying along darkening streets. 'You'll care when War comes,' he shouted after them; 'you'll care when bombs begin to fall, and when you breathe poison gas, and when you're starving and homeless. Then you'll care.' He looked up angrily into the sky, as though hoping at that moment to hear the drone of aeroplanes and see death raining from the air. 'They don't understand,' he said more mildly as we walked on, pitying them now, a pitying smile playing round his lips. 'They're like children.'

We went to Wilberforce's committee room. It was an empty shop with posters pasted on the window, and, in large red letters, 'Wilberforce This Time.' Inside there was a long trestle table loaded with leaflets. An elderly lady was seated at this table and addressing envelopes. She looked up at Wilberforce and smiled at him. 'Good evening,' Wilberforce said breezily. 'Good evening. How are things going?'

Without waiting for an answer he bustled about, looking at lists of names, turning over leaflets and posters, opening letters. The elderly lady made tea for us, and then resumed her addressing. Her blouse had a high collar, and she was dark and highly coloured.

Wilberforce, Miss Annerley, and I sat round a gas fire to drink our tea. We felt isolated in the empty shop and drew close together. Shadows passed backwards and forwards across the posters on the shop window, across 'Wilberforce This Time'. I watched these shadows and thought, 'Children of men, oh children of men.' As I watched I seemed also to be passing backwards and forwards, a shadow.

'What do you feel about them?' I asked Wilberforce, pointing to the shadows. 'You're their champion, I know. But what do you feel when you see them like that – shadows coming and going?'

'They're so pathetic,' Wilberforce said, 'so helpless. Their trust has been so often betrayed. If we let them down, my God if we let them down!'

'Don't include me,' I said. 'I'm helpless and pathetic, too. I've been betrayed again and again.'

We sat without speaking, and I went on watching the shadows passing to and fro, and thinking, 'Children of men, oh children of men.' I thought of Humanity, all the men who had ever been, were now, and would be; dark aboriginals and blond Europeans and yellow Mongols, every variety, and thought, 'As they are I am. We are all the same.'

'Have you ever,' I asked Wilberforce, 'felt conscious of being superior to anyone else, to an imbecile, say; or of being inferior to anyone else, to some rich important person, say? If it were a question of saving your life or someone else's, might it occur to you that yours was the more worth saving?'

'We must get on with canvassing,' Wilberforce interrupted. We went from door to door; knocked and waited, hearing footsteps rumble deep inside the house, then approach nearer and nearer, until at last the door was opened a crack.

'We've come on behalf of Mr Wilberforce's candidature,'
Wilberforce said. 'Vote for Wilberforce if you want Peace,
Better Housing, more Education . . .' He smiled ingratiat-
ingly, like a commercial traveller pulling Peace, Education,
Housing, out of his bag and extolling their excellence. He
travelled in Wilberforce. 'They don't know who I am,' he
whispered to Miss Annerley and me in the street outside, 'so
it doesn't matter my asking them to vote for Wilberforce.'

'Not know who you are!' I laughed. 'Of course they do.'

'You think so?' he asked eagerly. 'You really think so?' His face was joyful when I assured him I really thought they knew who he was.

We progressed slowly up and down long streets. Miss Annerley and I grew tired, but Wilberforce was tireless. His voice each time he said 'Vote for Wilberforce' was as fresh as though he had never said it before; and he waited at each door with undiminished expectation. When no one answered the door and the house was dark and silent, resounding emptily to his knock, he whispered 'Vote for Wilberforce' to himself, like a muttered Grace, and slipped a leaflet into the letter-box. 'One more street,' he said, 'and then we'll stop. It's late and they'll be going to bed.' He was angry at the thought of their going to bed. In bed and asleep they were beyond his reach. Their eyes and ears were shut in bed, and they could not see his ingratiating smile, or hear his ingratiating 'Vote for Wilberforce'.

'Do you love them,' I asked, 'stretched out in their dark corners, some alone and some clasped together, dreams flitting through their minds, and hopes? What dreams, Wilberforce? Peace, Education, Housing? Or dreams of sudden wealth, golden crowns and sparkling coronets and ermine robes and lovely women and fame and seeing all the wonders of the world?'

'It's the Cause,' Wilberforce said, 'not them or me as individuals.' His voice rose shrilly. 'I've seen a vision – these mean streets all swept away; air, light, culture, happiness, leisure, being made available for all, a better relationship between man and man, the removal of the haunting fear of War and unemployment and destitution.' He climbed on to a low wall and began to orate. The public houses were just emptying, and soon he had a little audience swaying slightly together as they listened to him. 'Comrades,' he shouted, 'I've been going all this evening up and down the streets you live in, and I've been shamed and angered by the dirt, the misery, the overcrowding, the want and privation I've found in them. It's filled me with shame to think of how easy

69

my life has been compared with yours, of the expensive
school and university I was sent to, the opportunities I've
had to travel and enlarge my outlook, when you have been
imprisoned in this darkness.' The faces listening to him fused
into one Face, swollen, somnolent, swaying gently to and fro
like an overgrown blossom on a slender stalk. This Face, as
Wilberforce dwelt on the wretchedness he'd seen that evening, became sorrowful. Large drops formed themselves in its
heavy eyes, and hung suspended. 'How long,' Wilberforce
asked with passionate earnestness, 'is this to be? The answer
rests with you. In your hands is the power to alter these
conditions. Will you use it?' Now the Face tautened. Anger
burnt away its tears. 'Yes,' it seemed to say, 'yes. Tell us but
how.' Wilberforce smiled. 'You want to know how?' His
fingers stroked the Face, caressing its leaden cheeks; his lips
approached its swollen lips. 'Oh beloved, you want to know
how? I'll tell you. It's so simple. All you have to do is to
follow me, love me, be me.' He was working to his climax, as
he had typing his leader. 'If you want your working and
living conditions to be bettered, and this cruel unjust social
system of ours to be scrapped and replaced by another, and
hope and joy and purpose to come into your lives, then –
then go to the polling station next Thursday week, go in
good time, the earlier the better, and mark a cross against
Wilberforce – he's your Man.'

He turned away, the light dying out of his eyes as it had
out of Margaretta Barfoot's and mine when we lolled together
among her coloured cushions. 'The apathy's so astonishing,'
he said bitterly. 'I can't understand it.' He was spent. He had
given himself, first in his leader and then in his speech. There
was nothing left. 'Sometimes I ask myself why I should
exhaust myself like this, why bother about them when they
don't bother themselves, why not just amuse myself.' His
arm sought Miss Annerley's. She drew close to him and away
from me. Wilberforce called a taxi and got into it with Miss
Annerley. 'Good-bye,' he shouted to me, 'good-bye. It's
been so nice seeing you.'

I weighed Friend against Wilberforce; I tried Friend's hat

on Wilberforce's head, and hung Wilberforce's hair like darkness over Friend's face and Friend's blond silky moustache over Wilberforce's anxious lips; I danced Friend and Wilberforce on the pavement in front of St Martin's-in-the-Fields. Friend was the Kingdoms of the Earth, Wilberforce was the Kingdom of Heaven on Earth. Wilberforce put down Friend from his seat and exalted Wilberforce; he sent Friend empty away and filled Wilberforce with good things. Friend rendered unto Friend the things that were Friend's. I walked for many weary miles between them. The road was dusty and the sun beat down, and I was thirsty. 'What's the matter with you, Friend?' I asked myself, and, 'What's the matter with you, Wilberforce?' The sun set crimson in the sky, and my heart melted. This was life, I thought – tremulous and uneasy as a leaf, passionate as the crimson sky, mysterious as the brown earth, and full of confused sounds like distant music. When the moon rose I thought, 'I know what's the matter with you, Friend, and with you, Wilberforce. You're not disinterested. The Kingdoms of the Earth and the Kingdom of Heaven on Earth are interested, but the Kingdom of Heaven Within is disinterested. Friend loves Friend, and Wilberforce loves Humanity – that is Wilberforce blown up, magnified, into Humanity and Humanity boiled down, concentrated, into Wilberforce. You're the same, Friend and Wilberforce – Friend in and Wilberforce out, then Wilberforce in and Friend out.'

Again I thought, 'Children of men, oh children of men,' seeing this time instead of shadows passing backwards and forwards across election posters, across 'Wilberforce This Time', shadowy hurrying figures with echoing footsteps and white faces which flashed past mine like sudden flashes of light. I felt a great tenderness for these hurrying figures, as though I knew them all intimately, all their troubles and hopes, all the circumstances of their lives. I wanted to take each one's hand in mine for a moment and press it. I had no fear of any, no grudge against any, no desire to use any for my own purposes. I knew that they and I were the same.

12

Gorging Small Print

I woke up in Bayswater. I stirred under blankets and recognized a window, a table, a wardrobe, a chest of drawers, a washstand, and two chairs. Sun poured in through the window. The air was still flavoured with tobacco smoke from the evening before. The sun which had awakened so much life into activity, birds to sing, plants to unfold and push towards the sky, tigers and cows to stretch themselves, insects to free their wings – awoke me. I got out of bed, washed behind a screen, and cleaned my teeth. Cold water brought a momentary glow to my face, like a red sun showing through fog and then hidden again. I looked down at my legs to draw on socks and thought: 'What is my life?' Those limbs with their covering of light hair – those limbs were mine, were me. I had sprouted them as a tree did branches. They had kicked their way out of my mother's womb, too weak and puny to bear my little weight; then strengthening until I tottered about on them, but still sagging and shapeless; then straightening, acquiring a shape, stockinged, trousered, gently stroked over, tangled with other limbs and untangled, growing sinewy and dry and lean, and soon to numb and chill and rot away.

As I put on my clothes garment by garment, drawing up the trousers, fastening the collar and tying the tie, I thought, 'What is my life?' My father turned towards my mother in their double bed, and I was conceived, and my mother's belly swelled, and, groaning, she pushed me into the world, and I was born. Then I found that I was living on a planet rolling through space, and that the stars littered profusely over the sky were other earths and suns, and that my days were numbered, and that I had a burning passion to separate myself in some way, as by being noticed or listened to or written about in newspapers and books, and another burning passion to merge myself in some way, as by burying part of my body in another body or by finding an identity with rocks and stones and trees; and I found that these two conflicting passions – to separate myself and to merge myself – tormented and bewildered me; and sometimes I abandoned myself to one and sometimes to the other, and sometimes thought I had eliminated one or the other, or comprehended both, but never had, except momentarily in one embrace, on one exquisite June evening when I wept and wept to see the earth so lovely.

I brushed my hair in front of a mirror staring in my own eyes and at my yellowing teeth and red moist mouth and nose projecting with little hairs growing down it like grass, and thought, 'What is my life?' coaxing myself for an answer, as Wilberforce had his audience – 'Oh please, what is my life?' then angry, gripping my neck and furiously shaking my head, 'What is my life?'

Now I was dressed and cool and determined. A day was in front of me. Other days had been wasted, but not this one. This day must be usefully employed. Lord Reading attributed his success to a wise planning of his time; I would plan my time wisely and become Lord Chief Justice of England and Viceroy of India. Wesley meticulously planned his time and sinners fell prostrate along his way; I would plan my time meticulously and lay sinners low. I planned my time – breakfast, then an hour's reading to make my mind quiet, then two hours' writing, ink smoothly flowing, lines evenly spaced, sheet following sheet; then a short walk and an abstemious lunch. As I sat planning, breakfast was brought in, and a newspaper. My planned morning that was to make me Lord Chief Justice of England and Viceroy of India, and to make sinners grovel and shiver and faint along my way, was an abstraction, soon obliterated by scrambled eggs, yellow as a sunflower.

I ate and turned over the newspaper. The columns of print gathered me up and swept me along, headlines like great breakers, smaller print a gentler swell. Things were happening in the world, and I must know what they were.

Otherwise I should get left behind. Straining to keep abreast, I marched in a torchlight procession, cheered beneath a balcony, rioted in Lahore, spoke in grave measured tones, bowed my head, smiled and looked troubled. 'Why is Titulescu in London?' I asked myself, and thought how naïve it was to take his word for it that he was just taking a holiday. Titulescu, I reasoned, did not undertake a journey to London for nothing. Not Titulescu. He must be canvassing support, holding conversations, receiving and being received. 'Sir,' I began, 'I was astonished to read in your columns . . . Surely it is obvious to anyone at all conversant with the facts . . . And I submit, Sir . . . Yours etc., P. Flammond.'

I read on greedily, gorging small print. A man had been found dead in his pyjamas. It was an inflammatory combination – Death and pyjamas, blood spilt and blood heated, Death and Lust. The deceased had vanished from his home some weeks ago and had last been seen in the company of a woman in a sealskin coat. What riotous weeks after methodical years! Which did he regret, the weeks or the years, as he lay dying in his pyjamas? I moistened a dry mouth – dead in pyjamas on the bathroom floor, and in the kitchen a meal for two with cigarette ends on the plates, and an empty bottle and unfinished joint; pyjamas his shroud and his ecstasy. She in her sealskin coat remembered the first time that ever he put them on – in a hotel near Victoria Station on a spring afternoon when the birds were singing in the trees, and sunshine dried the pavement outside their window, and Welsh miners went by singing 'Lead, Kindly Light', as though their hearts were breaking.

Reluctantly leaving the man found dead in pyjamas, I turned to book reviews. Mr Goring, I read, had arrived with his new novel, so why not I with mine? Sir Andrew Barlee, the novelist, had sailed for Hollywood, and I lingered still in Bayswater. A life of Moses was shortly to be published, and not by me – 'Recent events in Palestine and Germany lend an added interest to the great Jewish law-giver's astonishing career . . .'

There remained only gossip paragraphs and advertisements. The pace of my reading slackened, like a child getting to the end of a slice of cake. 'It is not generally known that Major-General Sir Frank Breighton-Jones plays the guitar.' I had not known it and now knew. I stared at advertisements – cigarettes to smoke, suits to wear, medicine to swallow, chocolate to eat, insurance policies to take out, and motor cars to drive. Languidly, I turned over the newspaper once more to see if some overlooked fragment remained, and then laid it aside, a crumpled empty skin with no fruit left.

I sat at the window smoking a cigarette and looking down at the street below. Its life washed backwards and forwards, as aimless as mine. It was me, parched like my mouth, stale like my breath. How many streets I had thus looked down on, how many cigarettes thus consumed! 'Street,' I thought, 'immune to the seasons, dying not in autumn, born not in spring, immortal street, gleaming in the rain like a river, melting in the heat of the sun, worn by innumerable footsteps, a channel along which life flows!' A housemaid shook out a doormat, beating it on the little patch of grass in a front garden and raising a cloud of dust. As she bent forward her skirt fluttered, and a milkman's and my heart quickened for a moment and our eyes strained.

The book Wilberforce had given me was called *The Idea of God* and was by Professor James Hurly. I turned over its pages, still marching in a torchlight procession, cheering outside a balcony, rioting in Lahore; still dead in pyjamas and sailing for Hollywood and writing a life of Moses; still marvelling that Major-General Sir Frank Breighton-Jones played the guitar, and smoking cigarettes, putting on suits, swallowing medicine, munching chocolate, driving motor cars; still Lord Chief Justice of England and Viceroy of India, and with sinners still falling prostrate along my way. I threw pennies to a lean man playing a violin in the street, and he stopped playing to bend down and gather them up. 'Erigena says that God is above all the categories, including that of relation,' I read. 'God, whether above or below all

75

the categories,' I prayed listlessly. 'Oh, incomprehensibility!' I groaned, preaching from the Woolsack, viceregal in the pulpit. 'Oh, incomprehensibility!' padding noiselessly after Titulescu, noiselessly dying on a bathroom floor after troubled sleep against a black sealskin coat, arriving and departing and picking up pennies in the street and – 'I am weighing my words. Mr Flammond's study of Moses is the finest piece of biographical writing of the century.'

The Idea of God was a desert, and I staggered across it, looking forward to the guinea I should earn with my short notice if worth it. 'Ruysbroek finely says,' I read, 'that as hunger presupposes bread so does Man's longing after God presuppose God.' Bread was born of hunger and the water-brook of thirst. Resting in the shade, reapers cut pieces of bread and carried them to their mouths with quick movements, and bowed down beside a water-brook to quench their thirst. Then, refreshed, with the sweat dried on their foreheads and their swollen veins subsided, they picked up their scythes and went out again into the sun. If there had been no bread there would have been no hunger, and if no water-brook no thirst. I hungered and thirsted, staring across the litter of the day's news and down into a grey remote street.

13

Along Cool Polished Corridors

Professor Hurly sat distraught in his study. Books lined the walls and were piled on little tables. He sat distraught among books, his face lined and unhappy, and his mouth set. He wore black clothes, and there was a small patch of damp on his collar where it touched his neck, and his hair lay damp on his forehead.

'Your book made a great impression on me,' I said. 'Some parts of it I shall never forget, as the part about . . . about hunger presupposing bread and therefore a longing for God presupposing God.'

He nodded grimly.

'At the same time,' I went on, 'there were parts I didn't quite understand, and that's why I thought I'd come and see you before venturing to review so important a book.'

'What parts don't you understand?' he asked irritably.

'Well, for instance, about God being above all the categories. I didn't quite understand that.'

He explained what being above all the categories meant. He reached down books and read passages from them, turning over their pages ravenously, like a hungry man peeling a banana. His voice was tremulous and faint, as though it hurt him to speak. It seemed to come from far away, from a deep cavern. He bent his head to within a few inches of the page he was reading, moving it along the lines of print. Spectacles with thick lenses enlarged his eyes and made the faint streaks of blood in them seem great raw wounds.

'I think I understand now,' I said gently. 'Please don't bother any more.'

'I'm going blind,' he said, and looked round bitterly at his books. 'It's reading in bed.'

I dreaded that he might spend his little remaining store of sight on explaining to me how God was above all the

categories, and darkness fall upon him in my presence.
'Don't read now,' I pleaded.

'It makes no difference – gradually, day by day, each day
a little darker than the day before, like days shortening in
the autumn; each day print a little harder to decipher,
until on a day I can't decipher it at all. Then I shall read no
more.'

He reached for more books, building them round him like
a barricade behind which he could crouch and fend off
darkness.

'Even if,' I said, 'longing to see God presupposes his
existence, how am I to see him?'

He let the book whose pages he was eagerly turning, fall.
The pits round his eyes deepened. 'I don't know,' he said. 'I
don't know. Perhaps I'll know when I'm blind, with nothing
to distract me – not even knowledge.'

'Do you believe in prayer?' I asked.

'I've prayed.'

Hour after hour he had prayed, when his alarm-clock
called him unwillingly from bed on a winter morning. He
prayed with his eyelids squeezed down and his head bent,
a forlorn figure. His prayers were too sincere to be answered,
like food too nourishing to be digested. They lay unanswered
about his study like dust, and heavy on his heart like unspent
passion.

'I'm afraid,' he said sadly, 'that the veil has scarcely been
lifted for me. I've had to do the best I could.'

Sometimes he had hoped for a palpable vision, mistaking
the first grey morning light for heavenly radiance sent to
lighten his darkness; looking at hands and feet for stigmata
as he rubbed himself ferociously with a harsh towel after his
cold bath.

He took me to see the Reverend Jewdwine, for whom, he
said, the veil had been lifted. Cool polished corridors led us
to the Reverend Jewdwine. He was sitting with a bearded
Indian and a Quaker named Dane in a little room. Their
chairs were in a row with the Reverend Jewdwine's in the
middle. A long black beard sprouted, silky, from his ruddy

cheeks and little tufts of black hair from his fingers. His eyes
were near and meek. He wore a pale green suit and yellow
shoes without toe-caps.

'We were discussing,' he said, 'pacifism in relation to the
doctrine of Ahimsa.'

The Indian rose from his place and spoke volubly in a
foreign language. The Reverend Jewdwine laughed gently
at his vehemence. 'He says,' he said, 'that non-violence is as it
were more than non-violence.'

'I mean,' the Indian said in English, 'that non-violence . . .'

Dane interposed. He said he believed in non-violence, as he
had shown in the War when he had gone to prison as a
conscientious objector. At the same time doubts had occurred
to him. 'I should like the guidance of other members of the
group,' he said. 'I cannot forget Our Lord with the money-
changers in the Temple. I'm just searching.' His voice had

been growing drier and drier as he spoke until it scarcely sounded it was so dry. His face and hair and high bare forehead were grey. Even his lips were grey

'I wish,' the Reverend Jewdwine said, 'that Bapu was here. He would explain everything. I shall never forget how he said to me one evening in Benares as he sat spinning, "Non-violence is a soul force. Soul is always non-violent. The soul of even a mad dog or of a rock hurtling over a cliff is non-violent." Perhaps – ' turning to Dane – 'that thought may be helpful.'

We walked together along more cool polished corridors. They were clean and fresh, and I scarcely dared breathe in them for fear my breath should remain, a little evil-smelling pocket of air, polluting their freshness. At lunch the Reverend Jewdwine took the head of the table. Dane scattered proteins from tins over his food and into his drink. When the Indian asked him, 'Mr Dane, what is your attitude to baptism?' he said he regarded every bath as a baptism, even washing his hands, and every meal as a sacrament. He had a room in the East End, and lived among the Poor. He lived quietly and industriously among the Poor, his grey forehead wrinkling, and singing a hymn every morning at six in a baptismal bath, and afterwards brewing a sacramental cup of tea.

'My young friend,' Professor Hurly said, indicating me, 'wants to see God. I'm afraid I wasn't able to help him much.'

'Have you seen God?' I asked the Reverend Jewdwine.

He smiled and stroked his silky beard, and gently nodded his head as though to say, 'Oh yes, I've seen God. I've seen God many times.'

'Do you believe in immortality?' I asked.

He continued smiling and stroking his beard and gently nodding. 'I remember Rabindranath saying to me once,' he said, ' "The pitchers are constantly emptied and filled, but with the same fluid." Perhaps that thought may help.'

'No, but I mean,' I shouted angrily, 'do you believe that you, Jewdwine, will exist as a separate individual for ever? that God made you, spinning your silky beard, dyeing your cheeks?'

My vehemence broke helplessly against his steely meekness. 'How ardent he is!' he murmured indulgently. 'It's wonderful to see – Youth confidently pitting its strength against Eternity.'

Professor Hurly's brow was agonizedly crumpled; Dane stared in front of him with his lean fingers tightly interlocked; the Indian's eyelids were lowered and his breathing regular.

'I'm not pitting my strength against Eternity,' I began. Then the Mystery broke upon me. We sat there, five of us, with legs and hands and eyes; we sat there, five of us, each alone in the universe, all alone, two bearded, three not bearded; we sat there, five of us, once fertilized eggs, microscopic, and soon to be stretched out, cold, our limbs leaden, lifted only to fall with a dead thud; stretched out, and never stirring, and nothing seeing, until we stank – five heaps of putrefying stench; until we mouldered away – five heaps of dust, and the dust scattered leaving bones, leaving nothing.

'Stop!' I shouted. 'We must die.'

Dane looked startled, but the Reverend Jewdwine still gently stroked his beard, and the Indian still sat with eyelids lowered and breathing regular. I seized the Reverend Jewdwine's beard, and pulled him close to me and stared deep into his meek eyes – 'You believe you are immortal? You believe you will exist for ever? In you is a certainty that henceforth and for ever there must be Jewdwine?'

His eyes were cloudy. I saw nothing in them. He seemed as I tugged at his beard to be nodding – 'As it was in the beginning, is now, and ever shall be, Jewdwine without end.'

'I shouldn't go quite as far as that,' Dane said. 'It seems to me that although the promise of some form of immortality is clear, its precise nature is uncertain. Something of us, for instance, is left behind in our work, and we live on in our children, and I like to think that love endures. All this represents a kind of immortality, doesn't it?'

I let go the Reverend Jewdwine's beard and marvelled at Dane's immortality. 'Where are your children?'

81

He sighed, yet he might have had children. That grey dry trunk might have sprouted fresh green shoots. 'Where is your love?'

Again he sighed. Who was Dane's immortal love? Whom had Dane loved?

Sighing – 'there's my work.'

He had scattered himself, immortal dust, over tenement stairways winding from floor to floor; he had squeezed himself, immortal ink, on to leaden words; he had vaporized himself, immortal sound, from platforms.

Sighing – 'there's my work.'

'Suppose no work,' I said, 'no children and no love. What then?'

'Then,' he whispered, 'then . . .'

I took his hand. It was dry like bark. 'Nothing? Only the Self twining its tortuous way from darkness to light – that's nothing.'

'You should come to India,' the Reverend Jewdwine said blandly. 'You really should. Come to Santineketan and let the Poet show you the way to peace. Every morning at daybreak parties of children sing happy songs. Teaching is by the direct method. An open-air theatre encourages the development . . .'

His voice found a well-worn channel. He spoke smoothly, easily. The Indian stirred and yawned. Professor Hurly said he had examination papers to correct, and the Reverend Jewdwine that he had to go to St Leonard's to deliver an address.

The Indian, Dane, and I returned along cool polished corridors to the room where I had first found them. We sat on the three chairs there in front of a grey radiator. How secret we were, hidden away! Looking up at a window high above us was like looking up from the depths of a well. 'Let us,' the Indian said, 'discuss the question of Freedom and Slavery.'

'Freedom,' I said, 'is to do what I like. I did what I liked with Margaretta Barfoot. I'm free.'

'I can't quite agree with you there,' Dane said. His voice

was as quiet and reasonable as ever. 'Limitations are set on the freedom of the individual in the interests of the community. For instance, I'm not free to let my drains smell.' He turned to the Indian. 'Isn't that so?'

'Smell is not smell,' the Indian said. 'Draining and not draining are the same.'

'I agree,' I said enthusiastically.

Dane was patient. 'I mean a very bad smell. It causes perhaps typhus. The people next door catch it. Then the people next door but one. There is an epidemic of which many die.'

'Dying and not dying,' the Indian said scornfully.

'Let me explain what I mean,' I said. 'I walk full of Lust along the Euston Road. I see Lust in swollen scentless blossoms clanging in the wind. Then, after a short discussion about whether anything can be done for German-Jewish refugees, Margaretta Barfoot and I among coloured cushions, blithely, blithely on her divan expend our Lust, and when it is spent blithely continue with our discussion about whether anything can be done for German-Jewish refugees.'

'There might be a child,' Dane said, agitated. 'The child might – I don't say would, get a poor start in life, contract disease, infect others.'

I laughed. 'Oh no, there was no danger of a child. Margaretta Barfoot saw to that. Our freedom was sterilized. It was sealed and sterilized, like hair brushes in a hygienic barber's shop. It was safe dead freedom. There was no danger of a child to get a bad start in life and perhaps contract disease, I assure you.'

'I should like,' the Indian said, 'to discuss the question of Love and Hate.'

'There is, of course,' I went on, 'another sort of freedom, unsterilized, unhygienic, unsealed. Oh Dane, oh Indian, another sort of freedom, a consuming fire.'

'If you don't mind,' Dane said, 'I'll join a few friends who are having a quiet time together.'

The Indian and I went with him. We sat in rush-bottomed chairs, and buried our heads in our hands. All round us were bent tweed shoulders and blond heads buried in pink hands. Occasionally a head looked up like a flower unfolding. Gold spectacles gleamed – 'let us think prayerfully of the states- men assembled at Geneva. That their decisions may be wisely and truly taken.' I too looked up – 'let us think prayerfully of the Lusts of the Flesh. That they may be guided aright.' The heads unfolded one after the other, like buds opening one after the other in a garden – 'let us think prayerfully of the Death of the Body. That it may be guided aright.' They dropped coins on a plate, at the same time singing a hymn. The ring of the coins on the plate broke through their singing like tinkling cymbals. I motioned the Indian to follow me out. As we went along cool polished corridors we heard them still singing, their voices strong and determined, the ring of the coins steady.

14

Eagerly He Showed Me the Stars

The Indian's name was Malik. He lived in Kentish Town. In the narrow front garden of his house there was a yellow cardboard sun, weather-stained, and a little pool of water with a lotus floating on it. His wife sat with us in the sitting-room. She was a large red-haired Danish woman with bare clumsy feet, and wearing a long mauve dress which was tight over her body. I addressed her as Madame. She brought in sandwiches and sweets on a tray, and I ate them. Malik did not eat. He hovered round the tray, like a bee round a flower, occasionally darting towards it but never settling. Madame played the piano and sang. Music was her life, she said.

'Your immortality,' I said, remembering Dane. 'Do you know Dane?' I asked. 'He's immortal. He will leave himself behind in his children and his love and his work.'

She laughed. 'He's got no children.'

'I know,' I said.

She went on playing, talking to me over her shoulder as she played. Malik moved restlessly about the room. He was dressed like Tolstoy in loose trousers and a loose shirt not tucked in and with a belt round it. His beard was like Tolstoy's, and so was his troubled brow; but he was shrivelled, shrunken. He could not fill out the pattern he had taken. Madame ignored him and tried to isolate herself with me. I feared her raw large feet pressing down the piano pedal and her raw large hands clutching at the keyboard, and followed Malik as he moved restlessly about the room.

'How do you come to be living here in Kentish Town?' I asked him.

He spread out his hands deprecatingly. 'I find myself here,' he seemed to say. 'It's my fate, as she is.' He took me on to the roof where he had a little platform arranged and a

telescope. 'I look at the stars,' he said. The wind caught his beard. He was a wild distraught figure looking at the stars through his telescope. 'Telescopes get more and more powerful,' he said. 'More and more is seen. My telescope – ' again spreading out his hands deprecatingly – 'is nothing.' Eagerly he showed me the stars, naming them. We were perched on our little platform and all round us was the universe. 'Chain-letters,' he said, 'are abominable.' He squatted on his haunches beside his telescope and brooded on chain-letters. 'When I get one,' he said, 'I destroy it, and sometimes I write protesting to whoever's sent it to me.' As he told me this it seemed heroic to destroy a chain-letter. He had worked out statistics proving that if everyone sent out chain-letters the post office would become choked in a few months.

'Let's start a crusade against chain-letters,' I said. 'Let's devote our lives to stopping them. We'll form a society for their suppression. We'll have headed notepaper – The Society for the Suppression of Chain-letters, the SSCL. We'll circulate literature, and hold meetings, and get into Parliament, and write in the newspapers. You'll be President, and I'll be Secretary. It's a Cause, and I'm looking for a Cause to devote my life to. On our death-beds we'll think, "Because of us there are no more chain-letters. We've achieved that with our lives – the suppression of chain-letters." '

I was eager to begin. He sighed. Perched on a little platform and all round the universe, the moon rising and pouring its soft light into space. 'In Florida,' he said, 'they're making a telescope two hundred times as powerful as mine.' He looked at his telescope with distaste.

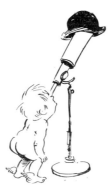

15

Blue-Print for the Good Life

Mr and Mrs Daniel Brett received me in their study. There were two desks, shelves of books, a clear space for striding up and down, and tall windows looking on to a lawn. Mr Daniel Brett was sitting at one of the desks, and Mrs Daniel Brett was leaning against the mantelpiece and smoking a herbal cigarette. She was taller than he was, and white-haired, with angry eyes and an arrogant mouth. He was rubicund and industrious, with a small round belly pushing out his waist-coat and short plump legs.

'We begin work,' she said severely, 'at ten. It is now nine thirty-five. Lunch is at one.'

'When we say we begin work at ten and lunch at one,' he said, 'we mean that we begin work at ten and lunch at one; neither earlier nor later.'

I had twenty-five minutes. There was no time to lose. 'I made up my mind,' I said, 'to look for God.'

Mrs Daniel Brett frowned, and Mr Daniel Brett grunted.

'We have no objection,' she said, 'to your indulging in spiritual exercises.'

'But,' he said, 'we see no reason why you should inflict them on us.'

'Hear me out,' I pleaded. 'I've abandoned that search. I see that it was hopeless and misguided. Now I want to plan. I want to draft the blue-print of a new civilization. Help me to draft the blue-print of a new civilization. Show me where to begin.'

'First,' Mrs Daniel Brett said, 'investigate.'

'Collect facts and arrange them,' Mr Daniel Brett said.

'What facts?' I asked.

'Where do you live?' Mrs Daniel Brett asked.

I said that I lived in Penge.

'Study,' Mr Daniel Brett said, 'the governing institutions

of Penge. Answer the questions, How does Penge feed itself? How does Penge amuse itself? and so on.'

'Find out,' Mrs Daniel Brett said, 'whether Penge is increasing in size or diminishing. If the former, find out whether it is due to an excess of births over deaths, or to migration. If migration, find out why and whence.'

'When I've finished with Penge?' I asked.

'Then,' Mr Daniel Brett said, 'extend the area under investigation. Take in the whole of London, then the Home Counties.'

'Until,' Mrs Daniel Brett said, 'you have a clear understanding of the structure of Society, how it works, its production processes, its cultural activities, its layers of population.'

'Then,' Mr Daniel Brett said, 'you will be in a position to consider how it may be improved, modified, perhaps drastically changed.'

Mrs Daniel Brett chewed her finger noisily, joyously. 'Then,' she said, 'you will be in a position to cut away dead wood, to abolish existing institutions which no longer serve any useful purpose, to devise new ones as and when they become necessary.'

I looked anxiously at my watch. 'Tell me,' I pleaded, 'the conclusions your investigations have led you to, and what in your opinion must be cut away, and what instituted?'

She strode up and down the room cutting away dead wood, and Mr Daniel Brett panted along behind her removing little branches which she overlooked. She cleared a great empty space. St Paul's Cathedral collapsed at her touch into a little heap of dust which the wind soon dispersed; the Houses of Parliament toppled over into the Thames and were no more seen; the Bank of England burnt like dry grass on a railway embankment leaving only a charred patch of ground. She emptied the universe of its content until it was only space with her voice resounding through it and echoing sibilantly in Mr Daniel Brett's. The Word was Word again as at the Beginning, and all creation. There was nothing but Word growing like coral, adding to itself until it

became a vast structure, sunny domes and caves of ice and caverns measureless to Man.

'People!' I shouted. 'Are people dead wood?'

'Man as producer, man as consumer,' Mr Daniel Brett said.

'People!'

Mrs Daniel Brett turned on me savagely. 'What do you mean – people?'

'Take a concrete case,' Mr Daniel Brett said. 'Suppose a demand for silk stockings. The demand is estimated; production and distribution are arranged accordingly; so many legs require to be covered with such a fabric, and are.' He was triumphant.

'Supposing,' I said, 'a one-legged woman.'

Mrs Daniel Brett looked at her watch. 'Three minutes to ten.'

'When we say ten,' Mr Daniel Brett said, 'we mean ten; neither earlier nor later.'

'Tell me,' I pleaded, 'about a new civilization.'

'If you are interested in our views you must read our books,' Mrs Daniel Brett said severely.

Mr Daniel Brett pointed to them, two shelves of books. He got up and ran his plump fingers over them, like a pianist running his fingers over a keyboard before beginning to play.

'You might,' Mrs Daniel Brett said, 'while you're waiting for lunch read our contribution to this symposium of views on what constitutes the Good Life.'

She handed me the symposium, and I sat in the garden with it open at their contribution – 'The Good Life', by Eleanor and Daniel Brett. The sun beat down, and a gardener was mowing the lawn. Through the tall windows of their study I could see Mrs Daniel Brett striding up and down, and Mr Daniel Brett sitting patiently at his desk. Their industry made me feel ashamed. 'How does Penge govern itself? how feed itself? how amuse itself?' Penge was remote, but Earth was near, a little freshly dug patch, like brown froth spilt on grass. How did Earth govern itself? I

93

wondered. How did its innumerable inhabitants – worms, insects, minute bacilli – manage their affairs? Were they increasing? or migrating? Earth as producer, I thought, making seeds sprout, awakening fertile desire; Earth as consumer, rotting vegetation and flesh; Earth amusing itself in riotous colour and fragrance, in the tiger's snarl and the nettle's sting and the bird's song and the thunder's roar and the moon's light. Now to cut away dead wood! I cut away the angry dart and the shrinking fear and tremulous fornication. I made old life bud new as coolly as old thought budded new. I regulated the seed's ardour, and reinforced the young shoot's frailty, and tempered the honeysuckle's passionate scent. I said to the bacillus, 'Be patient!' and to the worm, 'Take thought.' Then I looked at what I had done, and in place of Earth I saw principles, abstractions, un-responsive to the sun's heat, unthirsty for the rain's wet, unfearful of the frost's grip. There was death in my touch. I touched the sky and it unrolled like a blind; I touched plants and creatures and they died. Even the sun went out like a fused bulb, and there was darkness.

In this darkness I sighed for Penge. Penge was more manageable than Earth. I might refashion Penge without bringing down darkness and death. 'The Good Life by Eleanor and Daniel Brett' – was there good and bad life, or only life and death? Must the flower hate the bee because it stole its honey? Was there no more significance in the worm's life and my life than their own sustaining? The darkness I had made lifted. I sensed a Oneness in all the diversity round me, and this Oneness was irradiated with an inward glow of love. I saw a significance in trees budding and un-folding leaves and then shedding them, and in the gardener pushing his mowing-machine up and down the lawn, and in my own shifting moods and emotions; in all the activities of Man, in the whole range of Man's being. 'Life is the Good Life,' I thought, and picked up a handful of earth, and crumbled it, and put it back in its place. 'Life is the Good Life,' I shouted through their study window to Mr and Mrs Daniel Brett. They did not hear me.

16

Read, for the Day of Wrath is at Hand

I walked away from Mr and Mrs Daniel Brett over a little bridge across a stream and along a road. On either side of the road was a heath covered with stunted trees. The road was white and dusty. As I walked along black clouds gathered and the air became oppressive. I was full of fear and dread. What would become of me? I wondered; how should I meet my end? – clawing convulsively at life as it went out of my reach, regretful of spent time and spent passion. 'Who am I?' I shouted. 'What is this flesh that has withered on my back? These hopes that have died in my heart? These assertions? These appetites? These ecstatic moments? These moments of despair? This past stretching back and future stretching forward? These legs that carry me, and eyes that light me, and searching fingers, and male organ suddenly insistent to be buried in a female organ, and ears that hear and apertures that excrete? What am I?' I shouted, and thunder rumbled, and lightning flashed across the sky, and heavy raindrops glittered in the dust.

A car stopped, and Strode, who was driving it, offered me a lift. Attached to the car was a trailer full of books. We took refuge from the storm together in this trailer. I sat down on a dictionary and Strode on a pile of novels. Strode had a large white loose face, and wore a tweed suit and a hat with a wide brim. I told him that I had been visiting friends in the neighbourhood with whom I was drafting a blue-print.

'For a house?' he asked.

'For a new civilization.'

He whistled. 'A large undertaking.'

I agreed that it was a large undertaking. 'So many facts to collect and questions to answer. How does Penge govern

95

itself? How does Penge amuse itself, reproduce itself?'

'Why Penge?'

'Anywhere would do for a beginning. Or anyone. You, for instance. How do you govern yourself? How do you amuse yourself, reproduce yourself?'

'I don't govern myself or amuse myself or reproduce myself at all,' he said. 'I believe in Love.' His large white face was woeful. 'Love follows me wherever I go. It haunts me, sleeping and waking. I can't escape from Love.'

He shook his head woefully. Lightning illuminated the trailer's little window, and thunder roared round us. 'What I mean,' Strode shouted against the thunder's roar, 'is that I'm always longing and longing for Love, and it always just eludes me. I meet someone, at a party, say, and I feel it at once, a great warmth inside me – Love. We talk together, and there's that understanding, that perfect sympathy, that capacity for utter frankness, which signifies Love. Perhaps we go for a wonderful walk, a whole day in the country, hand in hand; or have a wonderful evening together, dining at a Soho restaurant, a little tipsy as we step out into the dark street and link arms at the theatre, scarcely seeing the stage or hearing what the actors say, waiting for afterwards when we get into a taxi, people and traffic and lights surging round us, but unconnected with them, alone in our Love. Such a moment I'm always waiting for, and it never comes.' He sighed. Thunder seemed to shake the trailer, and rain beat down on its roof. 'Edna, my wife, knows how I feel,' he went on. 'She's not jealous. She wouldn't have me refuse Love. It couldn't be right to refuse Love, could it?'

His earnestness was oppressive, like sealions at the Zoo begging for food. 'Edna is old,' I thought. 'Edna is faded.' I saw Edna, a grey-haired lean woman in beach pyjamas. 'Once with Edna, long ago – did it elude you then?' I asked.

'Long ago,' he sighed.

As he sat silent, thinking of how long ago with Edna Love had not eluded him, and how now they slept in their different rooms, sprawling through the black night and dreaming, he another Strode and she another Edna, youthful, flushed;

thus transfigured, sometimes even finding their way into one another's arms – as he sat silent, thinking of Edna, I looked at his books.

'Do you sell many?' I asked.

'Of the wrong sort, yes,' he said. 'The good stuff won't go at all.' He pointed to the good stuff – Bernard Shaw, Aldous Huxley, D. H. Lawrence, T. S. Eliot. 'The highest I can get them to go is Priestley, but what they really like is those.' He contemptuously indicated a shelf of novels with gaudy dust-covers.

'They're all about Love,' I said.

He indignantly denied that they were about Love.

The rain stopped and the sun began to shine again. We got out of the trailer and climbed into the car, and drove on to a village where we stopped opposite the church. Strode rang a bell and opened the back of the trailer to show the books which were in it. A few people collected, staring curiously at Strode with his short legs and wide-brimmed hat and white loose face. He made a short speech, pointing out that most people spent more on ties, let alone beer and the pictures, than on books, yet books contained the wisdom of the ages. Put it at its lowest – knowledge was power and knowledge was contained in books, so books were power. On a higher valuation, books spread enlightenment, progress, and civilization. 'Available for a few shillings,' he said, taking off his wide-brimmed hat with a sweeping gesture, 'enlightenment, progress, civilization.'

His audience drifted away. Windows which had been opened shut down, and children continued with their play. An elderly lady with a yellow wrinkled face asked if he had any books about David Livingstone, fingered a volume on Crime and Insanity, and bought a shilling edition of *The Return of Tarzan*; and a girl, hatless, and wearing sandals and an embroidered dress, came out of the Vicarage and asked Strode in a loud voice if he had any of Lenin's works.

'No,' Strode said, 'but,' eagerly, 'I've got all the works of D. H. Lawrence, including *Lady Chatterley's Lover*.'

'I've read all them,' the girl said scornfully, 'and I'm *sick* of them. Where's your Economics section?'

Strode showed her *An Intelligent Man's Guide to World Chaos*, but she waved it contemptuously aside.

'No Marx, no Lenin,' she said, turning away.

'I've got a Psychological section,' Strode pleaded after her. '*The Origins of Love and Hate; Modern Man in Search of a Soul.*' She went on her way relentlessly, and Strode, helpless and despairing, watched her close the Vicarage gate behind her. 'She's wonderful,' he murmured. 'Wonderful!'

We followed along a stream to bathe, and when we had found a place took off our clothes and splashed in the water. Afterwards, Strode sat naked among the roots of a tree with flies buzzing round him. His sprawling white body was still dented where suspenders and belt had gripped it round. 'I don't even know her name,' he groaned. 'They must know at the post office, but it'd be awkward to ask. She might be the Vicar's daughter, or she might be a visitor. I'd like to give her a book – Synge's poems, and write in it: "Before Marx was I am." That gets the point rather nicely, don't you think?'

'You're being haunted by Love,' I said.

He nodded sadly, stretching out his arms. He was like a large white fungus sprouting out of moss and roots. 'I'll write to Edna about it,' he said, and took a fountain-pen and writing pad out of the pocket of his coat, and with the pad resting on his bare knee began to cover sheet after sheet with sprawling writing. 'I never keep anything from Edna,' he said. 'I tell her everything.' He was so intent on his writing that he did not feel the flies crawling over him.

Later in the afternoon we stopped at a little lonely church on a hill. The rectory was beside it, and the Rector was mowing his lawn. He was an elderly man with white hair and a shrivelled face. His wife sat on a deck chair watching him, and knitting as she watched, darting her needles emphatically into the stitches. Strode and I looked over the hedge, and as the Rector approached us with his mower I said angrily, 'You're a clergyman, aren't you?'

'Yes,' he said, pausing in his mowing, 'I'm a clergyman.'

'What do you believe, then?' I asked.

He looked at me mildly. 'What do I believe? I believe in God the father almighty, and in Jesus Christ . . .'

'I know about that,' I interrupted, 'but what do you really believe?'

'I believe,' he said, 'why, I believe in God the father almighty, and in Jesus Christ . . .'

'Listen,' I shouted, stern and harsh, 'I'm looking for God.'

'Where have you looked?' he asked, smiling politely.

'Where have I looked?' I leapt over the hedge, folded my arms and began: 'Up and down the world, and in other hearts, and in my own heart.' Ah, I was a pilgrim, wearily trudging, travel-stained. Ah, I had trudged many weary miles along dusty roads, through crowded cities and empty deserts. 'I sat cross-legged in India meditating on OM, I watched the sun rise across the Nile and bowed down before its glory, listened to philosophers in Athens, and took up my Cross as I was commanded; I mortified my flesh, and in a black gown announced the eternal damnation of all predestined to be damned, and built great palaces and wove rich fabrics and poured out eloquence and passion to God's greater glory; I tore down the Bastille, brick by brick, and announced a new reign of universal freedom and brotherhood, and demanded the Vote and education for all; I became a millionaire, and owned newspapers, and endowed libraries; I held up my deformities to the sun and moaned for alms . . .'

I was so absorbed in this oration that I scarcely noticed when the Rector resumed his mowing, keeping the rows nearly parallel, and pausing when he reached the end where I was to murmur, 'How interesting!' or 'Really!'

'What am I to do now?' I asked insistently, following the Rector along.

'Really,' he said mildly, 'I scarcely know.' He was on the last row, and as he finished it he added, 'I hope you'll both stay for a cup of tea.'

We had tea on the newly mown lawn. It was brought out by a maid in uniform. There was a little spirit lamp to keep the kettle hot, and hot scones under a silver cover.

'I gather,' the Rector said, 'that you've travelled a lot.'

I said I had.

'You've visited the Holy Land perhaps,' the Rector's wife said.

I nodded.

'We've always wanted to go, but something's always prevented us. We're not likely to go now.' She smiled savagely, showing false teeth.

'You haven't missed much. It's a barren desolate land.'

'I've heard,' the Rector said apologetically, 'that in the spring the flowers are very beautiful.'

The brick walls of the Rectory were solid and ancient, and so were the silver teapot and milk jug; the lawn, mowed and rolled so regularly for so many years, was soft and thick like moss. How secure these two were! I thought, how sheltered! Foxes have holes, and so had they. 'You say you don't know what I ought to do now,' I said, raucous again, 'but you ought to know. It's your business to know. You're given this sanctuary to live in on the assumption that you do know. If you don't, what function do you fulfil? Why shouldn't you just be left like other old men to sit in parks and wait for death to relieve your relations of the burden of having to support you?'

'I say my prayers,' the Rector said, 'and I'll pray for you.'

The four of us strolled across to the church for Evensong, and the Verger rang the bell. He and the Rector's wife and Strode and I were the only congregation. The Rector prayed and read the lessons in a quavering voice, screwing up his eyes when he closed them. Sunlight made the colours of the stained-glass window behind the altar glow. Outside there was the confused sound of a summer's evening, and the Church itself was full of summer scents. The Rector turned over the pages of a large Bible resting on a brass eagle, and read about how God was a spirit and must be worshipped in spirit and in truth. These words had been spoken so often, innumerable tongues forming them, century after century repeated, sometimes roared, sometimes whispered, hiccuped even, sometimes almost flickering out and sometimes a burning and a shining light; now filled only with timid sound, like a large organ timidly played. They had endured, I thought. Truth endured and falsehood died. Truth was incorruptible, and falsehood, like flesh, had its span of life and then died.

Kneeling there together, the Rector, Strode, the Rector's wife, the Verger, and I, kneeling there together we sent up our souls to seek God's face, and knew for a moment without any possibility of doubt that Will and Appetite were unsubstantial. 'We're brothers,' I thought. 'Our common plight binds us together, like children in one household, and all involved in its good and ill fortune. Whoever is involved in this Mystery is a brother – that's everyone. If there were any-one unaware of this Mystery – expecting to become insipid, tasteless, savourless dust, and yet knowing Eternity – he would not be a brother, he alone.'

The Rector knelt on in his place after the Benediction. How strange a chance, I thought, that had dressed him in a white surplice to stand in front of an altar, with two candles, a brass Cross, and two vases of flowers, and each Sunday morning prepare on it the Body and Blood of Christ, and each Sunday morning and evening offer it a plate of money! So quavering a priest, so quavering a church, washed by Time as a shore by the tide, accumulating Time's deposit, scarcely recognizable, greed growing to it like thick ivy, abomination enjoying its shelter; so corrupt a church, yet miraculously passing on its uncorrupt Word as seed was passed on generation after generation, uncorrupt, by corrupted bodies.

'We're all brothers,' I said to Strode as we drove away. 'Lust makes us brothers. We're brothers in Lust and in Death.'

'I object to the word "Lust",' he said. 'If you say "Love" I agree. Love makes us brothers.'

He wanted to make me say 'Love', rolling it out as he did, woefully; but I would not.

'Brothers in Lust and in Death,' I repeated, and shut my

ears while, lolling over the steering wheel, pausing to motion cars to pass or to take a difficult corner, he explained the difference between Lust and Love.

As I sat thus with my ears stoppered beside him, I noticed that the countryside was changing. The grass became sparse and meagre, the trees deformed, and the air had a harsh acidic tang. Black against the evening sky there were tall smoking chimneys, and cranes, and spirals of swollen tubing. Soon we came upon slag-heaps and a desolate tram terminus. Level-crossing gates held us back like the bars of a cage. We raged and stormed, and made frantic restricted movements; at last were released and leapt forward into crowded streets, with bright shops and cinema fronts and cinema posters. 'Look,' I said to Strode, pointing to one of these posters. 'Love!'

In the Market Square among booths of socks and ties and pyramids of coloured sweets, Strode rang his bell and opened his trailer and began his speech about knowledge being power. Near him a man tied himself up with leather straps and then with frantic shouts and tormented movements untied himself. Amidst the shouting, the crowd's troubled movements, the darkness and confusion of little lights, Strode's speech was more passionate and urgent than when I had heard it before. 'Read for the Day of Wrath is at hand, read lest you be weighed in the balance and found wanting, read, only read.' Strolling from booth to booth, people paused in front of Strode and listened to him for a moment or two. Perhaps there might be something in what he was saying, they thought, fingering in their pockets the coins they had to spend; perhaps they ought to read.

I went over to listen to another orator in the Market Square. He was a vigorous florid man. Over his platform a red flag waved, shadowy except when a light caught it, and then blood endlessly flowing. He shouted and raised a clenched fist into the air, turning sometimes to look at the smoking chimneys and cranes and spirals of swollen tubing, dark shadows against the sky. This background seemed to inflame and inspire him; it represented the wrong that embittered him and the hope that exalted him. 'Destroy this Temple and in three days I will raise it up to be more glorious than before.'

He destroyed, as Mrs Daniel Brett had, only more arbitrarily and passionately. His destruction was more exhilarating than hers. He went with fire and sword and fury, exulting – 'We the downtrodden and oppressed, we slaves harnessed to greed and with nothing to lose but our chains, we the toilers – our day is at hand.' His audience stirred. It might be as he said. A sense of their wrongs came to them. They worked that others might be luxurious and indolent; they endured discomfort, even, when a war came, died, for what? – to perpetuate their bondage. A large car clanged its horn angrily, wanting a way made. Within it they saw a woman lounging, her face powdery, her eyes contemptuous. A chauffeur in a blue uniform was driving, also looking contemptuously at them, ready perhaps to beat them down like grass if they continued to stand in his way. Why not now? they thought – pulling her out of her black car, trampling her underfoot, making those arrogant eyes fearful, tearing those rich clothes to tatters, forcing the chauffeur to drive them ribaldly through the streets shouting and singing. Bitterly they stood aside to let the car pass, and stared full of hatred through its windows.

'And don't imagine,' the orator went on, shaking his clenched fist now into the sky, 'that the old gentleman up there is going to interfere. I'm not afraid of him because I know he doesn't exist. He's been invented to be a bogy man. We'll get rid of him easily enough.'

On the other side of the Market Square I heard Strode. 'Knowledge is power; and you, the People, in whom all power is vested, must have knowledge if you are to exercise your power effectually. Lord Reading attributed his success in life to systematic reading . . .' Three elderly women with placards advertising Peace fluttered near me, mutely appealing.

Was the orator perhaps right, I wondered, and Religion a cunning device, saints mortifying their bodies so that the

Poor might be persuaded to tolerate their poverty? The Rector, so secure, with so solid a Rectory and so restful a garden – he preached acquiescence, and well he might. Were security and solid Rectory and restful garden a reward for thus preaching? Did Christ, when he preached the blessedness of poverty and humility, all unknowingly act as the tool of the Rich and the Proud? Were my own obscure longings to see God and forget the World no more than an escape from injustice and cruelty which I was too weak and indolent to resist?

Inspired by the Orator, I looked backwards and saw all history as a pageant of greed. I conceived History materially – kings and priests and demagogues, poets, even, conspiring to justify Wrong, God their creature, knowledge and genius their instruments, faith a reed through which they blew.

'Workers!' the orator shouted. 'Workers!' There seemed a touch of malignity in his voice. He seemed to be angry as he shouted, 'Workers!' Why? I wondered, when he was the shepherd and we the sheep of his pasture.

'You mean us?' I asked.

'You!' scornfully, then with clenched fist turned against his own breast, 'I'm a Worker, I!'

His 'I' embraced all mankind. He had destroyed, and now raised up 'I'. This 'I' engulfed us. We no longer existed except in his 'I'. It filled the whole world, the whole universe.

'What about us?' I asked humbly.

He looked away from our white upturned faces into the dark sky, seeing his Vision there – tall chimneys spouting fire, wheels silently turning, power concentrated in a single switch, and his the finger to control it; mankind's finger operating through his; his the finger.

I turned into a side street, quiet after the turbulent Market Square. People stood about in little groups. Through windows I saw people in rooms; each window a room, like little numbered lockers. From a public house came people's voices, a confused murmur. Were these, as the orator had prophesied, to rise up in their wrath and sweep, a destroying, purifying flame, over the land? Were they to coalesce, mighty in their fusion, and then revenge? The Multitude, the irresistible Multitude, a lake in which many fished, lips which many kissed and tried to make salivate – Vote for me! Love me! Want this, spurn that! You in me and I in you.

The confused voices I heard were my voice. I lingered on the pavement and lived in each room. Though I fled to the remotest desert, or climbed the highest mountain, or lived in a walled prison; though I died and my flesh became dust, still I must walk these streets and live in these rooms and speak through these voices. Though I searched the dark jungle, not even there should I find a creature not myself; the black aborigine with his blunted cranium and I, one and indivisible – taking him in my arms and pressing my twisted lips against his full ones. 'Oh, my beloved, myself.'

There was no possibility of being solitary. Thus God had intended it. In the labyrinths of my own mind I was not alone; nor did the flame of Lust consume the Self, but swelled it up, like yeast swelling up dough.

'We're all in the same plight,' I shouted, 'all strangers in a strange land.'

One or two gathered round; others just looked up where they stood; behind me a window opened. 'You, too,' I went on, 'sometimes think, fearful and bewildered, "Yesterday I was born, tomorrow I die." You, too, feel Lust's insistence; your apprehensions come in crowds, and the world sometimes dissolves into nothingness in your eyes as in mine.'

They were menacing. Someone gave me a push. 'You shut your mouth,' one or two grumbled.

'Ladies and gentlemen,' I began, to reassure them, 'I am here tonight to ask you to give your votes . . .'

Now they were easier. They stood back.

'Comrades,' I began, 'you know what unemployment is; you know what hunger is; you know what it is to have to put up with bad housing conditions. If you want these things changed the remedy is in your hands. You have the Vote; cast it . . .'

'Hear, hear!' one or two shouted.

'May I suggest,' I went on, warming, 'that you become registered readers of the *Daily Express*. It's first with the news; it serves neither Party nor Interest; its sole object is to put the Truth, the whole Truth and nothing but the Truth before the Public (that's you); its motto is service; it costs only a penny.'

I took off my hat, and they began to feel in their pockets.

Strode and I made our beds in the trailer. He had for a pillow *The Intelligent Woman's Guide to Socialism*, and I *The Oxford Book of English Verse* helped out by a Cookery Book and a pocket edition of Shakespeare's tragedies. We lay side by side, and, supporting our heads on our elbows, read for a little while by the light of a lamp placed between us. I read a story of Tolstoy's about a man who had been wronged by another man and then forgave him. This act of forgiveness was so vividly described that I felt it in myself, a deep pang followed by a sudden light-heartedness. Strode read an essay by Havelock Ellis.

'I'm a Pagan,' he said as he put out the light. 'I believe in Joy in Living.'

'In Love,' I corrected.

'They're the same,' he said sulkily.

Moonlight coming in through the little window caught his face, intensifying its whiteness and making it look like an actor's made-up face. Every time I woke up in the night I saw his white moonlit face uneasily asleep, snorting and groaning. The air in the trailer grew heavy, laden with our breath's staleness and the smell of paper and fresh print.

17

The Adoration of Young and Beautiful Creatures for One Another

Our first stop the next day was at Beulah, a cluster of wooden houses in a valley with one larger stone building which looked like a church. Strode stopped the car by this building and began to ring his bell. He rang it vigorously, breathing in the fresh morning air. A woman in a loose orange-coloured dress came out of one of the houses followed by a man with a thin brown beard and wearing velveteen shorts. Strode had not bothered to put on his broad-brimmed hat or to brush his hair. He was dishevelled, with the buttons of his shirt unfastened. 'I know,' he said to the woman and man, 'that I'm speaking to the converted when . . .' He pointed to the opened trailer with its rows of books.

The woman smiled. Her face was lean, with a single deep furrow in each cheek and in her pale hair a single strip of grey. This gave her a geometrical appearance. 'Of course, we've got our Communal Library,' she said, 'which we try to keep as up to date as possible. Mostly, we depend on gifts of books from well-wishers, but we do sometimes get a few through commercial channels when we feel they're essential for the work of a particular group.'

Both she and the man were wearing sandals. The man had two hammer-toes, one on each foot. They took us into their wooden house for breakfast. We sat at an unpolished table and ate oat-cakes and fruit and drank thin coffee. There was a hand-loom in a corner of the room. The woman said that her name was Jeannie and that the man's name was Bramwell. 'We're together,' she said, looking at Bramwell, who plucked nervously at his thin brown beard. 'He does photography – Art Photography, you know.' As she spoke she smiled continuously; but her smile chilled. It was a cold, hard smile, painted on her face like a clown's smile.

Beside the window there was a child in a long pram. It was well grown, and must have been about fifteen years old. Its face was empty of all expression. It had rich golden hair and blue eyes, and its cheeks were tanned by the sun. Sometimes it made a faint burring noise, and often smiled, showing fine regular teeth. Jeannie took the child a glass of milk, holding the glass to its lips and slowly tilting it as it drank. Her face softened as she did this, losing its geometrical rigidity, melting. When the child had finished drinking she stroked its rich golden hair and it burred contentedly. Everything about it was neat and clean. 'When it also has a thin beard!' I thought, and hurriedly asked, 'What is this place?'

'Well,' Jeannie began, 'we're a community. That's obvious, isn't it? You might even call us a Religious Community, only we're mixed' – she looked smilingly at Bramwell, who did not smile back – 'and have, naturally, no connection whatever with any sort of Church. We hold our goods in common; our unions' – again she looked smilingly at Bramwell – 'are free; our worship draws elements from all religions and follows none. Today, for instance, is a Festival dedicated to the adoration of young and beautiful creatures for one another.' Once more she looked at Bramwell, not smiling this time, eyes hard, mouth contracted.

'How wonderful!' Strode interrupted – 'adoration of young and beautiful creatures for one another! How wonderful!'

'There are other festivals,' Bramwell said. It was the first time he had spoken. His voice was high-pitched and irritable.

'We shall pile flowers on an altar dedicated to Love and Youth,' Jeannie went on, 'and dance and sing; and the Sage will speak to us, and the Mother bless us.'

'Oh!' Strode said, taking both her hands, inarticulate. 'Oh!'

'I've got some developing to do,' Bramwell said. I followed him, leaving Strode and Jeannie talking eagerly

together. In his Dark Room, Bramwell lit a little red lamp. He looked sad in that subdued light. His sandals and velveteen shorts were pathetic, like an old woman's lingerie.

'Tell me,' I whispered, 'friar quaver, semiquaver, demi-semiquavering quaver, where's the punk?'

'Our original intention,' he said in his high dejected voice, 'was to abolish Money and Marriage. This was what attracted me, since I had reached the conclusion that Money and Marriage were the source of all misery. For that matter, I think so still. I think so more than ever,' this savagely.

'Have you abolished Money and Marriage?' I asked.

'We've had to compromise all along the line,' he said sadly. 'First of all we didn't handle money at all. In travelling for instance, we went on foot and relied on being given food and shelter in return for work. What happened was that people either asked us for money or offered us money. When we told them we'd decided to do without money because it was the source of all misery they didn't understand. I remember a clergyman offering me a shilling. "No," I said, "no, I don't want it, I want food and shelter, but not money. I've sworn never to handle money again." He thought I was mad.'

'Never mind,' I said, wanting to comfort him, 'you tried. Few even try.'

His face was haggard and woebegone. 'We tried and we failed,' jingling coins wretchedly in his pocket.

'What about marriage?' I asked.

He began to walk agitatedly up and down the Dark Room.

'We've compromised there too. It's true we don't register our unions, but are we free? – we are not. I've been with Jeannie seventeen years and twelve days now, and

I couldn't leave her even if I wanted to. I don't say I do want to, but I couldn't even if I did. That's the point – *I couldn't.*'

'Why?' I asked.

He paused in his agitated walking up and down the Dark Room and said piteously, 'I really don't know why. All I know is that I *couldn't.* If I ran away she'd find me out, or I'd come back of my own accord, like a murderer coming back to the scene of his crime. If she went away I'd go after her.' I saw him by the dim red light tugging at his thin beard, a Knight of the Woeful Countenance, and imagined him long ago setting out, so hopeful and exhilarated, a ruck-sack on his back, *Leaves of Grass* in his pocket, bicycling, his calves exposed to the sun and wind – 'These preparations being made, he found his designs ripe for action, and thought it now a crime to deny himself any longer to the injured world that wanted such a deliverer; the more when he considered what grievances he was to redress, what wrongs and injuries to remove, what abuses to correct and what duties to discharge.'

'Bramwell,' we heard Jeannie calling. 'Bramwell!'

Bramwell looked startled. 'We must go,' he said, 'and pile flowers on an altar dedicated to Love and Youth.'

We joined a procession following behind an old man with a venerable white beard. His long white hair was parted in the middle, and he wore an orange robe and had garlands of flowers hung round him.

'He's the Sage,' Jeannie whispered to Strode. 'Isn't he lovely.'

The Sage led us to a little wood where there was an altar piled with flowers round which we danced hand in hand. With one hand I held Jeannie and with the other a plump woman with two thick blonde pigtails hanging from a tall witch's hat. As we danced the Sage led us in reciting 'L'Allegro'. Jeannie's voice was resonant in my ear: –

> Come, and trip it as ye go
> On the light fantastick toe . . .

When we had finished dancing the Sage exhorted us to be happy, to rejoice in the life that flowed in our veins, to satisfy and not repress our joys and desires. 'He who desires but acts not, breeds pestilence,' he said, and, 'Energy is eternal delight,' and –

> Abstinence sows sand all over
> The ruddy limbs and flaming hair:
> But Desire Gratified
> Plants fruits of life and beauty there.

While he exhorted us the Mother stood by his side, dressed in white, a white flower in her hand. She was a dark elderly Frenchwoman with a lined shrewd face. When he had finished she fetched him his coloured cubes, and he sat down cross-legged under a tree and built them into a pyramid. 'It's a philosophy he's working out,' Jeannie told me. 'The cubes are emotions, and he's building them into a Harmony. When it's finished it will be the Harmonious Life.'

We scattered two by two, except Strode who had no partner. He stood disconsolately alone and eyed the Mother. She smiled grimly at him, and he turned away muttering that he had letters to write. Sprawling on the ground in the shade of a tree he wrote a long letter to Edna, his wife. I scattered with the plump woman in a witch's hat. 'I'm Sheeba,' she said tenderly, 'and you're the Fairy Man – for today. Tomorrow,' gaily, 'who cares about tomorrow?' We passed Jeannie and Bramwell. They had unclasped their hands, and Jeannie had let down her pale hair and was singing –

> Tibby hey down, down,
> Tibby ho down, down . . .

Bramwell looked irritable.

'Fairy Man,' Sheeba said, 'let's sit down.' I sat down and leant my head on one of her large breasts. There, bewildered, I rested. 'Let me admit bewilderment,' I thought. 'Let me admit that the circumstances which have brought my head to rest on this large breast are incomprehensible.' I belonged nowhere, came from nowhere, and was going nowhere; I was a piece of flesh twitching like a horse's flank when flies settle on it; I was a tormented piece of flesh, and that was all I knew on earth and all I needed to know.

'Fairy Man,' Sheeba whispered, 'Fairy Man!' and gently took my head off her breast and put it against a tree-trunk. The bark was hard where her breast had been soft, formless, folding over me like a wave. My cheek against the hard bark, I watched her take off her clothes, garment after garment, until her immense pink body lay naked on the naked earth.

18

Mrs Angel on the Embankment

High up in a little pulpit like a crow's nest Father Boniface was preaching. On the wall behind him there was a black velvet cross. Except for the little pulpit, the church was in darkness. It might have been empty, so silent was the crowded congregation, listening intently to Father Boniface, scarcely breathing. Light shining on him from above picked out his lean face and black eyes and close-cropped dark hair growing low on his forehead. He was wearing a black monk's habit with a white cord tied round his middle.

His voice broke and his hands gesticulated. He evoked white tormented limbs and blood spurting up as nails were driven into them, the crimson of blood on a body's whiteness, vinegar squeezed on to a parched tongue, a groaning lolling head and patient sad eyes, anxious disciples, despairing mother, shrieking multitude, a fateful night rent suddenly with echoing claps of thunder and flashes of lightning which froze shouts on startled lips and illuminated faces suddenly apprehensive.

A shiver swept through the congregation – 'That's the most momentous scene in the world's long history, that the moment to which all creation had been leading up, its fulfilment. The stars had looked down for how long, waiting, waiting; the sun had risen and set and the green earth renewed itself how many times in the expectation that at last God would become Man and Man become God. Think of it, oh think of it – God Incarnate dying that you and I and all men might live. Are we to refuse this blessed gift of life? Are we?' He stretched out his arms and leant back his head; then knelt down, burying his face passionately in his hands, his broad shoulders shaking.

The organ thundered; the congregation rose and, dazed, began to sing; the lights went on one by one. 'I know that my

redeemer liveth,' I sang, not knowing. The spell was broken,
the vision shattered – like opening a door and breathing cold
night air after waiting, heart on fire, for the maid to clear
away coffee cups (that the moment the stars had waited for,
looking down and waiting, in expectation of which the sun
had patiently risen and set and the earth renewed itself
innumerable times); then scattering clothes and crawling,
one shirted, one chemised, about the thick hearth-rug.

'I know my redeemer liveth,' I sang, not knowing. 'After
all, it *was* a momentous scene,' I reasoned. 'Look at its
consequences, two thousand years of consequences, the Archdeacon. After all,' I reasoned, 'what does it matter what
happened, who died – a megalomaniac with flashes of genius,
a saintly imbecile, a third thief? There were still the consequences, the two thousand years, the Archdeacon. After
all,' I groaned, singing.

I walked despairing, along the Embankment. I longed to die. 'Death,' I whispered, 'death,' like a lover. 'Oh that thou wouldst hide me in the grave,' I prayed, 'that thou wouldst keep me secret.' I wanted death to come upon me gently, like nightfall, to feel death creeping over me as darkness creeps over the earth, gradually melting me into nothingness, gradually obliterating me, and I peaceful in a twilight between being and not being. A little forlorn crowd was staring at the lights of ships and barges as they drifted by, envying their silent inevitable movement, their release. Faces furtive and aimless looked down on the Thames thinking, 'Night must pass and then day must pass, Time must pass.'

'What is everyone looking at?' an elderly lady with a large beaked nose and hair falling in strands out of her hat howled in my ear. It was Mrs Angel. Her withered cheeks were flushed. She too looked down at the Thames, but angrily, as though there were secrets to be torn out of its dark impassivity or pleasures to be enjoyed rolling on its sedate surface.

'We're only looking at ships and barges drifting by.' I said.

'Oh, I thought there might be something.' She turned away, and we walked up and down the Embankment together, she taking long disjointed strides and breathing in noisily through her nose. 'When I saw you all staring I thought something must be happening,' she said.

'Nothing's happening,' I said. 'It's only that we've nothing to do. We don't belong anywhere. We're destitute.' She gripped her purse tightly and drew her lips together. 'Poor souls.'

'We watch the Thames because it suggests escape – little streams merging in a larger one and that in the ocean; a ship fastened to a quay, bustling, alight, with noise and lingering embraces, then loosed and gliding away, a distant light, nothing.'

117

'You mean death?' she asked, shuddering.

I nodded.

'I don't want to die,' she railed, her eyes flaming, blood-shot at the corners. 'There's so much I want to see and do and so little time. I haven't seen the Niagara Falls or elephants pounding through the jungle. I haven't seen the Taj Mahal by moonlight.' She paused and added, 'There's a place in Prague, I've heard, where they make you young again with monkey-gland.'

I saw her gorging monkey-gland, taking great mouthfuls, stuffing it into her mouth with both hands and fragments falling down her dress like crumbs.

'You're young,' she said enviously. 'You've plenty of time. I'm old.'

It was a reproach – 'You're young.' I felt ashamed. A night like this, I thought, ought to be full of enchantment for me. I ought to take deep exhilarated gulps of air. The stars and the misty river ought to delight my senses. 'You're too old to love death,' I said, 'and I'm too young to fear it. Let's die together, then.'

She sprang away, horrified, as I stretched out my arms for her.

'To cease upon midnight with no pain,' I went on, 'clasped together, your shrivelled empty breasts against my uncovered ribs; your shrunken stomach against mine, still rotund; fingers interlocked, lips glued, eyes staring into eyes. Come.'

I raced after her along the Embankment, but she was too swift for me. Her age was swifter than my youth. At last I gave up the chase, and sat down beside her on a stone seat. She sat there ready to flee again. 'I daren't even sleep,' she said, panting, 'let alone die. I'm always afraid that if I go to sleep I might never wake again. How do I know the world won't end while I'm asleep, and I just lie on waiting, waiting for someone to come and call me? What certainty is there that if I close my eyes the Niagara Falls will still be when I open them again? The Midnight Sun might flicker out like a candle while I'm sleeping and be lost to me for ever.'

I got up to go. 'I'll wait and see the sunrise,' she said. 'I've always wanted to see the sunrise over the Thames.' Eagerly she watched for the first streaks of grey in the dark sky, tearing at them when they came, counting them over like a boarding-house proprietor counting over knives and forks and spoons after the evening meal had been washed up.

19

Expense of Body

I left her waiting, and went away to write to Strode. 'Dear Strode,' I wrote:

I took my wife for a holiday to Alexandria. I'm devoted to my wife and she's devoted to me. We've got two children named Peter and Anne. They're at Dartington Hall now, so its possible for us to get away. 'Beatrix,' I said to her, 'you need a change, we've got the money for my "Whither Europe?" articles, so why not you and I go off to Alexandria. Just you and I together. It'll be like old times. Flavell says it's wonderful in Alexandria, lying in the sun on the beach, carousing by night, eating raw onions and drinking thick Cyprus wine.' She agreed that it was a good idea, and I arranged to do an article or so en route to help out the "Whither Europe?" money – "What Next in Egypt?" I thought might run to eleven guineas, and then something light and short, on "Lotus-eating" say, that I'd easily be able to place. The sea voyage was not enjoyable. We didn't expect it to be. Neither of us likes sea voyages. Deck games bore us, the other passengers irritate, we tend to eat too much and so get liverish. The first view of Alexandria, however, enchanted us. There was a golden beach, and white houses and hotels among trees, and a general air of gaiety. 'Isn't it wonderful,' I said to Beatrix, taking her arm (we'd been a bit on each other's nerves). She pressed my hand against her ribs and agreed. Our hotel, the Universe, was not one of the expensive ones. It had been recommended to us by Mrs Angel, who, as you know, travels a lot on surprisingly little money, and sketches. In many ways we like it better than the ones on the Front. It was quieter, and the food was admirable, though, of course, plain, and perhaps somewhat mono-

tonous. The only disadvantage was that the back rooms
(we had a back room) looked on to a half-finished house.
Though no work was being done on it the builder's debris
was still lying about, and seemed to collect flies. Also, we
had a double bed, which we don't care for at the best of
times but which on hot nights we find insufferable. On the
first morning we went down to the beach. How lovely it
was! We danced into the water hand in hand, swam about
till we were tired, and then stretched out on the warm
sand. I felt exhilarated. This was to be a real holiday.
Time would cease to matter. 'What's the time?' I asked
Beatrix nonchalantly. 'Ten o'clock,' she said. Still three
hours to lunch, I thought, and bought a newspaper, and
went through it, the sun's glare making it difficult to read,
and the paper soon yellowing. There were local Greeks and
Italians on the beach as well as visitors like ourselves. I
kept glancing at the women's brown bodies and languid
sensual movements. Supposing, I thought, I were lying
here alone, how my blood would warm! how bold would
be my glance and how merry my smile! 'They're all
rotten with disease, I've heard,' I said bitterly to Beatrix.
Beatrix and I began to dart venomous looks at one another.
What was going on inside our minds was – 'I'm being
deprived of pleasure and it's your fault; you can't give me
any pleasure and so you shan't have any.' I went for a
little stroll, picking my way among sunbathers, glancing
furtively here and there. 'Everyone's so ugly,' I muttered
to myself. Bodies, as I watched them, swelled and blistered
in the sun; rouged lips on a brown face were like sores,
and the tang of cosmetics made me wince with disgust.
'Let's try and find a lonely part of the beach,' I said to
Beatrix. 'All this' – pointing round angrily – 'is horrible.'
We plodded along through the sand looking for a lonely
part of the beach, hot, our mouths dry, sand on our hair,
and did not find one. At lunch we had a bottle of wine. I
chose it because it was less expensive than hock, which we
should both have preferred. It was a coarse Italian wine,
and left sediment in the bottom of the glass. We managed

to finish the bottle, and then felt drowsy. So, after a cigarette, we went up to our room and lay down on our double bed. There, indolently and half unconsciously, we coupled, breathing wine and tobacco-flavoured breath into each other's faces. Afterwards, Beatrix went away to the bathroom and I looked out of the window at the half-finished house, flies buzzing round my head and occasionally settling. Then I forced myself to settle down to "What Next in Egypt?" and felt better.

20

Swallowed Up with Overmuch Sorrow

In a confessional box marked 'Father Boniface', I waited, trembling and my heart beating, like waiting in cold sheets for a bed-fellow. As I waited I muttered prayers – 'Help me! Guide me! Save me!' There was an acrid scent of incense in the air. I waited and waited, praying, 'Give me a sign!' I wanted a crucifix to glow as though with fire, or the lips of a Madonna to stir, or blood to drip from a stone Christ's wounds. My prayer was unanswered. I heard no sound but of voices mumbling at a distant altar, and saw no vision but of candle flames flickering under coloured images.

'Father, I have sinned,' I began. My sins, which had so often haunted me, eluded me now that I wanted to recite them. I grasped at them to offer them to Father Boniface, and they burst like bubbles and were nothing. 'Father, I have sinned.' Had I? What was sinning? 'Father, I have been unhappy.' That at least I could sincerely say; and perhaps being unhappy was sinning. 'Father, I have sought and not found, I have asked and not been answered,' I wailed, pitying myself. A little paper under my eye provided a classification of sins for the use of penitents. Had I been covetous? it asked. Yes I had. I had coveted. Had I committed adultery? 'Father, I have committed adultery.'

The first letter of the question was illuminated, and above it a little picture of a crucifix with a contrite figure bowed down beneath it. 'Father,' I whispered, 'I used to go in the afternoons when Hartshorn was developing photographs in the cellar. There were two white doors, one the front door and one at right angles to it leading into the bedroom. This bedroom door used to be left open for me, and when I'd finished in the bedroom I'd go to the front door, ring the bell and ask to see Mrs Hartshorn. The servant would say

that Mrs Hartshorn was resting, and tap on her door telling
her there was a visitor, and Mrs Hartshorn, inside, would say
that she would come soon. When she came I'd stand up to
greet her, and she'd ask me to take a cup of tea; and we'd be
sipping tea and chatting and smoking cigarettes when Hartshorn came up from the cellar with his photographs, blinking
in the light and holding up his photographs for us to admire.'

As I described this adultery to Father Boniface the harsh
scent in Mrs Hartshorn's bedroom mingled with the incense
in the air. It made me want to touch up the picture of my
sin – thus I crept in, looking upward to see if anyone from
the flat above was watching; thus she awaited me, and thus,
listening for footsteps from the cellar, we embraced; thus she
straightened my tie, and walking out through the garden
thus I felt the sun beat down, ripening my flesh like an apple.

I waited in vain for some sign of Father Boniface's presence.
Perhaps I had mistaken for his the footsteps of someone
shuffling up the aisle. I tried to reckon up my sins: 'I have
broken my beloved's heart and she has broken mine, I have
contaminated flesh with spirit and let spirit poison flesh . . .'
What was the total of my sinning? 'Father, I have been
unhappy.' I returned to that, my fundamental. Others might
be happy; the circumstances of life allowed of happiness; but
not I. I was like a cripple watching the whole-of-limb at play;
they danced and ran and climbed and wrestled, and he, a
cripple, watching, felt the same urge, but knew himself to be
maimed and apart. My part was to watch, sometimes envious

and sometimes reconciled, sometimes even hugging my incapacity; in the world but not of it, of the world but not in it. I left the confessional box, my sins unconfessed and unrepented of.

It would be easier, I thought, to write to Father Boniface. Speaking words, moist warm tongue forming them, making sounds and immediately afterwards hearing them like a frightening echo, was more painful than writing. I could be brave and frank, sitting silent and alone, and making marks on paper. 'I heard you preach,' I began, 'and it filled me with a sense of being a lost soul, so much so that walking along the Embankment afterwards I suggested to Mrs Angel, who was waiting there for the sunrise to paint it, that we might end our lives together. She, however, refused this offer. Far from wanting to die she bitterly resented the numbering of her days, and would gladly have availed herself of any means of extending them. Then I thought it would be a relief to confess my sins to you, so I went into your confessional box and knelt there, and my sins came thronging round me. I tried to sort them out and enumerate them, but without success. "What is sin?" I asked myself, and did not wait for an answer. The blessed feeling of being spotless that I had longed for did not come to me. I did not walk out from the church door into the street purified and at ease, but with the same horrors flitting through my mind, the same load of unhappiness bowing me down. Perhaps you can help me.'

21

Father Boniface

Father Boniface was shifting manure, his habit hitched up and displaying underneath, a pair of grey flannel trousers with braces going through the loops of pants. I helped him with the manure. On his suggestion, we decided who should push each barrow-load by tossing up a shilling. He did this tossing up half defiantly, as though to insist that being a monk did not prevent him from being a man of the world and a sportsman. It embarrassed me each time he took the coin out of his pocket and sent it spinning into the air.

'You've got doubts?' he said. 'That's your trouble, I take it?'

'It's not so much . . .'

'I've had doubts myself,' he interrupted 'plenty of 'em in my time. I had to stay here and pray for eight years before my doubts went. Eight years!'

'Even to doubt,' I said, 'presupposes some belief. What am I to do who am so void of belief that I cannot even doubt?'

I said it mechanically. At that moment it did not worry me that I was void of belief. I felt no burden of unhappiness, no longing not to be. The insincerity of what I said made me emphatic – 'What does it signify, my life, your life, your eight years of praying away doubt? What does history signify with all its aimless bloody conflicts? What the travail of innumerable individual spirits, battling with their appetites, vainly struggling to give a form to the formlessness around them and within? Why was I born and why shall I die? Tell me that. Time's aimlessness and Eternity's mystery – between the two I falter and lose heart.' I was walking unsteadily alone with a load of manure. The falsity of this outburst made me irritable. 'All meaningless,' I taunted, pointing up at the sky; 'all meaningless,' pointing at my own breast. The barrow toppled over, and I sat beside its contents repeating irritably: 'Why was I born and why shall I die?'

Father Boniface looked pained. His brow crumpled, and the corners of his mouth twitched, like a child beginning to cry. We walked up and down the garden. It had been raining hard in the morning, and now the sun shone through a haze of cloud. The damp earth clung to our boots, making our feet leaden; and the branches of fruit trees watered us when we brushed against them. Though it was summer and warm, there was a feeling of autumn, a slowness in the air. No quick thoughts came to me or quick sensations. 'Father,' I said to break the silence that had come upon us, 'I have been unhappy.'

'For eight years,' he said as though talking to himself, 'I prayed.'

I saw him praying for eight years, days slipping by as he knelt doggedly, like a battery being charged; unaware of the tumultuous world and unaware of his own tumultuous flesh. The peace of it! I thought.

'What did you pray for?' I asked.

'I hoped that others would come and join me,' he said. 'None came.'

'I'll join you – ' eagerly. 'We'll pray together for another eight years.'

Doggedly praying, should I not then forget the weariness, the fever? Would not peace descend upon me then as I had thought of death descending, like darkness blurring the Self's harsh outline, merging discordant cries into deep silence? I wanted to begin at once, I wanted to kneel down then and there on the muddy earth.

He shook his head irritably. 'God has revealed another purpose now. He has sent me into the highways and byways to save lost souls – you, for instance. You wouldn't be here if you hadn't heard me preach.' He quickened his pace until it reminded me of Mrs Angel's as she walked up and down the Embankment waiting for the sunrise. His footsteps were quick and nervous. 'What do you think of the Church?' he asked. 'It's in a poor way, isn't it? It requires, don't you think, someone to revivify its witness, another Francis of

Assisi or Loyola, Wesley even?'

'You,' I said.

He looked at me earnestly. 'You really think that?' his voice excited, words sharp and hurried. 'I was a curate in a fashionable church, and much sought after, especially by women. Even now – I have to keep my hands in my pockets.' He put his hands nervously in his pockets, rattling coins in one of them. 'I've got many gifts, you understand. People said I'd have made a great actor or politician or writer. I was urged to exploit my gifts. Then I saw the danger, and came here, and for eight years . . .'

He paused. How long they were, those eight years! How laboriously they had passed, like slow cows passing through a gate! A bell began to ring, and we went to the chapel. Three monks were already kneeling there. Father Boniface showed me to a place and took his own. The chapel was grey, with damp stone walls. We knelt on stone. The light was grey and cold. Father Timothy, the Superior, read the Office. He read through his nose, the words moistened and swollen as they passed through it, emerging heavily, like a tennis ball after being in damp grass. When the office was finished we knelt in silence, with no sound but Father Timothy's heavy breathing. This was where Father Boniface had done his eight years of praying. I watched him now, motionless, eyelids lowered, features immobile, like a death-mask, and wondered what thoughts were passing through his mind, whether with a pang of excitement he was still turning over the possibility of becoming another Francis of Assisi or Loyola or Wesley; thinking of hushed, expectant crowds, persecution that only helped his ministry, stones that miraculously missed their mark, clenched fists raised and impotently dropped; summoned urgently to Downing Street and Buckingham Palace, looked to for practical as well as spiritual guidance.

No prayers came to me. I only wanted one of the monks to leave the chapel so that I might leave, or at least to get up from his knees and sit so that I might sit. They stayed as they were, I watching them anxiously, like looking out of a railway carriage window for a familiar landmark that meant the end of a tedious journey; listening attentively to Father Timothy's heavy breathing and hoping to detect some irregularity in it preparatory to his shifting his position. They all four might have been frozen in their places, stone like the floor they knelt on. I remembered Mrs Angel's horror of going to sleep for fear the world should end while she slept, and she lie on for ever in her bed waiting to be called. Perhaps the world had ended now. Perhaps Time had stopped and Eternity come to pass, and I was fated to kneel eternally, and listen, prayerless, to Father Timothy's heavy breathing, and watch four monks as they prayed with stony faces.

Father Timothy rose clumsily to his feet and left the chapel. The rest of us followed him, Father Boniface remaining for a while alone. He had most prayers to say. The refectory had once been a farm kitchen. It had low rafters with hooks in them for sides of bacon. An anthracite stove stood in the middle of a large open fireplace. Father Timothy took the head of the table, and Brother Amyas read aloud while the evening meal proceeded. His voice was quiet and insinuating, his face pale, his eyes near together and his lips compressed. He obviously liked reading aloud. It made him feel important, as though he were conducting a service, and a priest instead of just a lay brother. He read about how the soul had three properties – an essential imageless bareness; reason, a mirror-like clearness reflecting eternal truth, and a spark, the soul's tendency to seek out its source. He did not understand what he was reading, and we, his listeners, did not attempt to follow, yet the words as he read them were somehow comforting, like the wash of a quiet sea at night. When the reading was finished Father Timothy broke silence. He was very different from Father Boniface, sprawling and amiable, with disorderly wisps of grey hair and little eyes misted over.

'Are you an artist?' he asked me. It was like asking a woman uncertain about her charms whether she attracted men. I said I was not an artist, and suddenly remembered having heard of him as I walked along the Front at Hastings with Miss Muskett. 'Father Timothy advised me,' she had said, 'that I ought to sever my connection with the Girl Guides,' her footsteps uneven because she wore on her left foot a boot with an enlarged sole, on the other a frail shoe. 'Who is Father Timothy?' I had asked, but she had refused to tell me, blushing and looking confused, like an Indian woman avoiding speaking her husband's name.

'I spend my holidays sketching, and sometimes do the scenery for Nativity plays,' Father Timothy said, sighing. I saw him before he became a religious: plump, velveteen-jacketed, with a loose black bow and distraught hair and coarse features.

Father Boniface took me upstairs to his room when the meal was over. It was a little whitewashed room, with an iron bedstead, and a chair and table. I sat on the bed. It had a board for mattress.

'Do you wear a hair-shirt as well?' I asked.

He nodded and showed it me underneath his habit, sensual, like a glimpse of underclothes. On the table were piles of letters. He pointed to them – 'Every day they come, from all sorts and conditions of people. Here's – ' picking one up – 'one from a Princess begging me to see her.' He let me see the coronet on top of the notepaper. 'Here – ' picking up another letter – 'is one from a typist. She writes that my preaching has changed her life, and asks me to accept a gift, a gold safety razor. Now what – ' laughing – 'can a monk do with a gold safety razor?' He opened the leather case the safety razor was in, took it out, fitted it together and played with it. 'If I send it back it'll hurt her feelings, and yet buying it must have made a hole in her savings.' He smiled, and immediately afterwards looked serious again. 'Tell me your difficulties.'

'Father,' I said, 'see desire trembling on my lips, hate and envy glittering in my eyes. I want to be pure of heart and see God.'

'I am the door,' he quoted in his vibrant voice. 'By me if any man enter in he shall be saved, and shall go in and out, and find pasture.'

'Tell me what it means.'

'I'm preaching a sermon on it next Sunday at Eton,' he said. 'I shall begin by describing the life of nomadic tribes wandering up and down the desert with their cattle. What are they looking for? – always for pasture. When they find it they pitch their tents and are at ease. Sometimes mirages

delude them. They think they see green grass and trees and sparkling water, and approach eagerly, and it is only yellow sand.' He was pacing up and down the room, making gestures, exalted. 'So it is in the world. The world is a desert, too, and all of us bewildered souls constantly seeking pasture. How are we to find it? . . . There I shall pause, stretch out my arms so, repeat the text – "I am the door . . ." and, speaking slowly, ask: Are we to turn away from this, the only door admitting us to the pasture we need? Are we to turn away when our Blessed Redeemer has said, "Knock and it shall be opened," and when to make us heed His words He died on the Cross? Oh, think of that death. That the most momentous scene . . .'

His eloquence flowed into the well-worn channel of the sermon I had already heard. Now his words were more confident, his passion and gestures bolder, like an actor changing from a new part to one he had played many times before. I ceased to listen to him, and when the chapel bell again rang I said that I would take a stroll instead of joining him at evening prayer.

From a beanfield I saw the lights of the chapel where the five monks were again at prayer. In the distance, and by moonlight, it looked more like a farmhouse than a chapel. The rich scent of the beanfield hung in the still air. Darkness was full of the moon's radiance. I felt tears warm on my cheeks, and whispered, 'I, too, am to know happiness.' Was this, I wondered, at last a prayer? The five monks kneeling were remote, pitiable figures; their chapel with its altar and tall white candles, a toy; the psalms and prayers they repeated had no more substance than old leading articles. This was God's love, and I, an atom in its composition, partook of its nature. Evil was only being separated from it, existing alone; death only being reabsorbed into it. 'Whether there be prophecies, they shall fail,' I thought; 'whether there be tongues, they shall cease; whether there be knowledge, it shall vanish away; but this remains – God's love glowing, radiant, at the heart of all creation.'

22

Evil Entered into Me

I felt disinclined to go back to Father Boniface. His pale earnest face and bright dark eyes filled me with repugnance now; and I dreaded hearing his sermon again and praying in the grey morning with four forlorn monks, Father Timothy or Father Boniface in flaming vestments giving each other Christ's body to eat and blood to drink, while Brother Amyas mournfully blew incense on them.

Walking along a main road, with telegraph wires moaning overhead and the lights of motor cars flashing past, I soon felt tired and dispirited, and turned into a café attached to a garage. There were three or four round tables and blue wicker chairs. The tables had holes in the top so that on fine days they could be used out of doors with coloured umbrellas attached. A woman made coffee for me, warming the pot, boiling milk, setting out digestive biscuits on a plate. She had a swelling in her neck. Her neck bulged unexpectedly after leaving her blouse. Above this bulging neck her face seemed particularly lean and gaunt, bright eyes burning out of its leanness, thin hair neatly arranged, mouth set. As I drank my coffee she knitted, fingers agile in their movements, as hard and bony as her needles.

'I've just had a vision,' I said.

She nodded without surprise.

'I saw God's love permeating all creation, shining out from within it.' Some of the happiness I had felt still clung to me, like spangles after a Christmas party; but already the memory of it was growing faint.

'Are you perhaps one of the Saints?' she asked.

I said I was not. 'And you?'

'It's ten years ago today since I went up to be sanctified,' she said. 'Mr Snowden was preaching. He was describing how the Holy Spirit would destroy all the little maggots like

135

jealousy, temper, and greed eating away at each one of us; and it came to me that I must go up. No one had persuaded me. I'd never seriously thought of going up myself, though I'd seen plenty of others sanctified. The Tabernacle was crowded, as it always is when Mr Snowden preaches, but it seemed like I was all alone. I'd never felt so alone before. I went up and knelt down, and Mr Snowden laid his hands on my head, and the Holy Spirit entered into me, and I cried for gladness.'

She spoke eagerly, like a wife describing her wedding years afterwards when her youth had faded; showing the wedding group, telling how nervous she had been, recalling little dramatic incidents. Her face was animated and her eyes sparkled.

'Of course, my life was quite changed. Before I'd been fond of my glass of beer and my bit of fun. Don't think I was a goody-goody.'

She had, I knew, said it all many times before. Her testimony had been given many times publicly and privately. It had taken shape slowly, like a verger's lecture on his church. Knowing this did not, as with Father Boniface, make me impatient and uninterested. Sincerity enlivened her words. 'This deep, simple sincerity,' I thought, 'is the essence of all truth. It is the essential ingredient. Give it me! Give it me!' I prayed.

'It meant,' she went on, 'staying behind when my husband went drinking. He liked to spend his evenings in a pub, and for me to go with him. Not that he was a bad man. It was just his nature. When I wouldn't go with him he was angry. The first Christmas after I was sanctified I refused to have any drink in the house. He said he'd never passed such a miserable Christmas, and in the evening went off by himself. I walked up and down the street after I'd put the children to bed not knowing what to do and praying for guidance. All our Christmases before had been happy times, and the Devil put it in my heart to wonder if I was doing right. As I passed by the Two Brewers he came to the door with a glass of beer in his hand and beckoned me in. I prayed, oh, how I prayed!

and God gave me strength to turn away; and I went to the
Tabernacle and had the Second Blessing there. After that he
tried to have me certified. He said I was mad – ' smiling –
'but I was as sane as you are. Then I found out he was going
with other women, and at last he left me. I've brought up the
children, and I'm thankful to say they've turned out well.
The eldest boy is in the Post Office,
and without any persuasion from me
has been up to be sanctified; the girl
is married to a good man, and the
youngest boy has just passed his
matriculation.'

She looked round complacently at
the little café, at the garage adjoining
with its illuminated petrol pumps, at
bars of chocolate and cakes under
their glass cover, at the till registering on a roll of paper the business
she did.

Evil suddenly entered into me and I saw her swollen neck like a red fungus, an immense piece of raw flesh, pulsating, soft. Her cheeks were dry and angry, her mouth cruel, her bright eyes hard. I wanted to hurt her, to kick over her illuminated petrol pumps, smash her till and scatter the money in it, bring down my fist on the glass cover and scatter splinters of glass over the cakes and bars of chocolate under it.

'Supposing,' I said, starting up, 'he came back, now, this moment, the door opening and he standing there, flushed with beer, smiling, his hand outstretched to take yours, reminding you how you once loved him and of the nights you spent in each other's arms when you were first married, swearing he loved you still, only you, and that he'd found other women tasteless and so had made up his mind to come back to you, his only love.'

Her swollen neck was throbbing violently. She looked distracted. 'After all,' I thought triumphantly, 'her husband was right to try and get her certified.'

She pointed at me, shouting, in her shrill clear voice, 'A visitation of the Devil.'

I drank my coffee, and got up, and asked her how much there was to pay.

'A shilling,' she said, her lips pressed tightly together.

I paid the shilling and went.

23

A Child is Born

That night I dreamt that a woman was waiting for me in a room. She was about fifty, plump and red-haired. There were many rings on her stubby fingers with long reddened nails, and large green ear-rings swayed heavily when she moved her head. As she waited for me she moved about the room, fingering a grand piano, smoothing out mauve curtains, her black velvet dress creased at the back from sitting down. There was a heaped-up log fire in the grate, and the walls were covered with oil paintings all alike. One over the fireplace was of a young Negro with pouting lips and holding a white flower in his hand. The windows looked on to mountain peaks covered with snow and touched with the sunset's glow.

The woman began to play the grand piano. I looked in at her playing, but she was so absorbed that she did not notice me. I stood there in a black hat and long black coat looking in and smiling. When I stopped smiling I felt still round my mouth the creases where the smile had been. 'Ah, you've come,' the woman said, looking up. I took off my black hat and kissed her hand. She patted my cheek. 'We were expecting you earlier.'

'The roads were bad. *Comment ça va avec la petite?*'

I spoke French in a laboured stumbling way, but still kept raking round in my mind for French words and phrases, getting them ready beforehand, like preparing for an examination.

'*Maintenant ça va mieux; mais c'était terrible – ter-ri-ble!* Two doctors, three nurses. *Ça coûte beaucoup, vous savez.*'

She gave this last remark – '*Ça coûte beaucoup, vous savez*' – particular emphasis. I understood why, and hurriedly asked: 'She suffered?'

'*Ter-ri-blement.*'

'Where is she now? Can't I see her?'

I was ardent, impetuous. My impetuousness brushed aside the two doctors and three nurses and their cost. 'Take me to her, take me to her!' I was neither to hold nor to bind. *Ça ne coute rien, vous savez.* How young I looked, a mere boy, insisting, 'Take me to her, take me to her!' and brushing aside all other considerations, as two doctors, three nurses, their cost.

The woman went upstairs, and I took off my long black overcoat, sat down, and lit a cigarette. It occurred to me that I had not asked about the baby, not even whether it was a boy or a girl. Several times I had said to Palmyre, 'Have a child by me, do,' and once, climbing back into bed, cold, she had asked, 'Would you really like me to have a child by you?' 'Yes,' I had answered passionately, 'yes!' remembering the gurgling of her syringe that I had heard from the adjoining bathroom.

'*Venez!*' the woman shouted, and I bounded upstairs, two stairs at a time, ardent and impetuous again.

Palmyre, lying in bed, was as much made-up as ever. On the table beside her I saw among medicine bottles powder and lipstick and a mirror. Beneath the make-up her face looked drawn, and wore a sulky petulant expression. I kissed her hand and looked down on her tenderly, and asked, not to be behindhand this time, 'The baby?'

She shrugged.

'Are you feeding it?'

'No, thank God.'

'A pity.'

'*Pourquoi* – a pity?' savagely imitating the way I said 'pity'.

Embarrassed, I picked up the book she had been reading, Dostoevsky's *The Possessed* in French. The room was growing darker. We had often sat side by side in a darkening room, the darkness awakening passion. I knelt down and put my face near to hers. Her eyes slowly filled with tears, large dark eyes become liquid, overflowing, like a wound overflowing with blood.

'I'll get a divorce,' I said vehemently. 'We'll marry. It'll be wonderful.'

'Fool!'

'Then why are you crying?' I asked helplessly.

'*Tu ne comprends rien.*'

We both laughed.

'I was looking at your new picture,' I said. 'It's very good.'

'*Le Nègre?*' she asked eagerly.

'Yes. Who is he?'

She smiled, and I felt a violent pang of jealousy. 'I'd like to see the baby,' I said.

'You can ask the nurse' – indifferently.

I got up to go and look for the nurse, jealousy awakening my parenthood; then came back and knelt down again by her side. She looked at me fixedly; and I turned away my eyes from her gaze, the room quite dark now except for the firelight.

'I've got to leave tomorrow,' I said. 'I'd hoped to get at least a week off, but it's impossible.'

Her dark eyes melted again. I put my face against hers, her cheek impassive, her mouth still.

'You don't want me to go?'

'*Tu ne comprends rien.*'

I woke up with this cry: '*Tu ne comprends rien,*' in my ears.

24

Appleblossom

Coloured birds were singing in a large gilt cage in Dr Apfelbaum's waiting-room. I and two other patients turned over the pages of illustrated periodicals and listened to their song, occasionally glancing surreptitiously at one another. We sat in red chairs with shining metal arms. On the floor was a thick grey carpet on which footsteps showed as on sand. One of the two other patients was a lady in a tightly cut tweed costume, the skirt split at each side, and stiff black hairs growing round her mouth. Particles of powder had collected on these hairs like dew on grass, and, as she turned over glossy pages and listened to the coloured birds, her mouth from time to time trembled convulsively, as though she were trying to say something but could not form the words. The other patient, a man, had a large moustache that sprouted energetically. He kept twisting and turning a suede shoe in the air.

'It's like a little restful garden,' I said, 'not like indoors at all.'

The man glared, the lady smiled.

'Is it your first visit?' I asked her.

'Oh no,' she answered, 'I've been coming to Dr Apfelbaum regularly for some months now. He's wonderful.'

Her eyes glowed lovingly in her red cheeks.

'He's done so much for me,' she went on, 'so much.'

The man's moustache began to agitate, like water reeds in a gale. 'Central Europe,' he began, 'when I think of Central Europe . . . the blindness . . . the foolhardiness.' Agitation overcame him. He sat weeping over Central Europe in Dr Apfelbaum's waiting-room, his suede shoe more than ever agitated. 'I'm Sir Launcelot Asprey,' he said. 'I contested Hartlepool South in the last election, making Central Europe the main plank in my platform; but, of course, no one would

143

listen. When it's too late they'll see. When it's too late.'

'There, there,' I soothed. 'Don't take it to heart. Tell me about Central Europe. I'll listen, and I'm sure this lady will too.'

He jumped up energetically: 'There,' arranging an *Illustrated London News*, 'is Hungary, and there's,' pushing a vase of flowers into position, 'Transylvania.'

I had to leave him before his explanation had gone any further because a nurse in a white overall summoned me to Dr Apfelbaum.

As I went through the door I heard him vehemently continuing: 'There's Bessarabia. Now imagine for a moment . . .'

Dr Apfelbaum was sitting behind a wide expanse of desk. His clothes were immaculate and his person so clean and fragrant, face lightly powdered, and a blue shadow over it, hair and eyes deep black, gold wrist-watch nestling among thick hairs, each finger with its black tuft, gold fountain-pen and writing pad in front of him.

'Your name?' he asked. 'Age? Married or single? Children? . . .' He dealt brusquely, absent-mindedly, with such trivialities.

'Now,' he said, fixing a penetrating gaze on me, 'tell me.'

'Tell you what?'

He smiled as though to say: 'That's not a new one on me. I'm quite used to that.'

'Appleblossom,' I said, 'I'm unhappy. Make me happy.'

He rubbed his hands. 'Why not? We should all be happy. I'm a great believer in happiness. But – ' seriously – 'what form does your unhappiness take?'

'It makes me want to die. "In love with easeful death" I keep saying over and over to myself, or "Where the wicked cease from troubling and the weary are at rest".'

He looked grave and made a note with his gold pen. 'When you cross the road sometimes do you feel a desire to get run over?'

'No,' I answered, warming up, 'but sometimes when I'm going along on top of a bus or a tram, stopping and staring, you know, especially just at nightfall on a wet October evening, lights coming out and electric signs, everyone's step hurried, the streets gleaming like a river's surface with lights reflected in it – then, Appleblossom, I sometimes wish that the bus or tram would go on and on for ever, and I never arrive at my destination.'

'Most interesting.' He made another note.

It pleased me to be interesting. I already saw myself immortalized when selections from his case-book were published. 'W. said that sometimes when he was riding on top of a bus or tram on October evenings he hoped that the bus or tram would go on and on for ever, and he never arrive at his destination . . .'

'Not only that,' I went on eagerly, 'but when such a mood comes upon me and I happen to see a horse, even a floundering old cart-horse, I feel a great burning love for it. "Horsey," I whisper, and the other passengers on the top of the bus or tram stare at me, "Horsey, I love'oo," for some reason reverting to childhood speech; sometimes not being able to form words at all, but only able to point at the horse and coo, my knees curling up as though I were back in my mother's womb.'

He showed me to a couch under the window, telling me to lie down on it, and shut my eyes, and drain off the contents of my mind. I lay down on the couch, and he took a seat behind me. Though I could not see him I knew just how he was sitting – head bent a little forward, expectant, interested, like an elderly Nonconformist on his first visit to a night club waiting for the cabaret to appear on the dark and suddenly silent dance-floor.

I was staring into a mirror examining my face – there the nose with its faint veins and tremulous nostrils; there teeth, yellowed, some loosening, a few gaps; there lips, speaking, kissing, snarling, and cheeks already corroded, some time to be eaten by worms and reveal the bare skull, then dust; within, the tongue lapped by digestive fluids, breath taken in fresh and expelled stale, brow and eyes reflecting passing moods, cunning, amorous, uplifted, or still and inert as October ponds.

'Appleblossom,' I began, 'you're in my mind. I keep thinking of you. Although my eyes are turned away I keep seeing you – your paleness, the blue shadow on your face, black cloth with a pinstripe covering you like a skin, the cold serenity of your black eyes. I should like to break open the cage in your waiting-room and set the coloured birds in it free, scatter all your notes and papers to the wind, set fire to your apparatus and your curtains in art shades, leaving you naked on the naked earth.'

'Go on!' he said smoothly.

'I'm wondering, Appleblossom, if, supposing instead of me a lovely woman on your sofa, the sort of woman you must admire, fair and slim, soignée, outspoken, well-bred, babbling erotic dreams – wondering if then a shiver might not strike under your black pinstriped skin, your gold fountain-pen tremble as it wrote. Would it? Would it?'

Soundlessly laughing, he waited.

'I'll begin at the beginning. I'm having my portrait painted. I'm lolling on a mauve bed, the easel in front of me, reading about Gauguin's death, how he limped with swollen suppurating legs through marshy vegetation, liquid fiery green. The artist leans over me, spilling her rouge like blood on my face. How desolate that is! How false! Then, Apple-blossom, I'm orating, with a million patient, upturned faces spread out at my feet, and how desolate and false that is! Then I'm writing, invoking words, snatching at passing shadows, striding up and down a room, beating my head against the wall, shouting and grimacing, and that's desolate, that's false too. At last I'm in a walled prison. I shake the massive iron gates. I think I see, but can't be certain, a crack of light as I shake them. Oh, the hope it gives me! Oh, the joy I feel! The joy passes, the hope dies.'

Dr Apfelbaum saw me genially to the door. 'Quite promising, quite promising,' he said. 'My secretary'll arrange another appointment. We'll get on to something positive next time. We've cleared the air.'

25

Into the Dangerous World

I leapt into the dangerous world. In a crowded room, with typewriters tapping and tobacco smoke rising like a morning haze, I had my corner where I scribbled, praising the mighty in their seats, scorning the humble and meek, ebbing and flowing with great ones, quick to fasten on to success, quick to detach from failure, sometimes uncertain, then waiting, cautious, not knowing whether to snarl or flatter, until a sign was given – an approving nod, Friend's back arched. The many men so beautiful – these were my province. I knew them, their habits and recreations, how much money they had, their hosts of friends; I spoke to them on the telephone, softly, softly – 'Oh Sir John, you play golf, you love music, you are rich, you've seen men and cities'; I turned over cuttings about them collected in an envelope and thumbed from being so often turned over – 'Sir John is a familiar figure at symphony concerts, Sir John is tall with a grey moustache and Leslie to his friends, Sir John has travelled widely and has a correspondingly wide outlook'; I stroked Sir John's grey moustache with a soothing gentle motion, and whispered in his ear, 'Sir John, dear Sir John, true Sir John, faithful just Sir John, oh Sir John.'

Then on Fridays I signed a book, and was given a little sealed envelope with four five-pound notes in it. Joyously I unfastened this envelope and joyously counted over its contents, the four flimsy pieces of paper, now mine. Lovingly I fingered them, frail and delicate. They were power. They lightened my darkness, making what had been incomprehensible comprehensible. Because of them I understood. The newsboy's passionate shout, the prostitute's smile, the coloured balloons hawkers floated in the air, the hurrying footsteps of men in black, all became comprehensible. The four flimsy pieces of paper were pleasure, ease, whatever I wanted. Lovingly fingering them, my step was confident and my heart unafraid.

From Friday to Friday the dangerous world was mine –
passing taxi-cabs, and gay companionship, and food and
drink and fine clothes and bodies eager to be unwrapped. I
sat, lordly, breathing fragrant air while my nails were
trimmed and polished; stood before three mirrors while a
tailor knelt, measuring, chalking, smoothing; took the chair
which waiters hurried to offer me, ate the food they brought,
tossed them, too, their small reward as Sir John tossed me
mine.

'After all,' I wrote to Dr Apfelbaum, 'I shall not require
another appointment. I see now what was the matter. I was
like a man staring in through the window at a ball. Now I've
got an invitation, go confidently to the door, am announced
and welcomed, find a partner, dance and forget the cold
uneasy street outside, the other face staring palely in as I
once did. Thus, my dear Father Appleblossom, there is no
further need for me to confess and get your absolution.
Every Friday an absolution is given me in a little envelope,
and my sins all drop away, perhaps to return the following
Thursday, but then a little wait, and lo! another absolution.'

To celebrate my cure I took Dr Apfelbaum and Mrs
Angel out to dinner. We sat at a little table, a shaded lamp
lighting our faces and our plates, and ate and drank and
smoked. 'Who would have thought,' I said to Dr Apfelbaum,
'when I lay on your sofa draining off the contents of my mind
that relief would come so swiftly?'

He smiled, inscrutable.

I raised a glass. 'How to repay?'

'It was little enough I did,' Dr Apfelbaum said.

'No, you did much,' I insisted. 'You showed the way, and,
unaided, I should never have found it.'

'Perhaps we doctors don't know as much as is sometimes
thought,' he said. 'Sometimes a cure comes suddenly, sometimes after long waiting, and sometimes not at all.'

'Your friend, I take it, is a distinguished doctor,' Mrs
Angel said to me.

'I can never be sufficiently grateful to him,' I answered,
looking affectionately at Dr Apfelbaum. 'He ministered to

my diseased mind. You remember that night on the Embankment when I asked you to die with me; dissolve and quite forget – well now, thanks to him, I want to live, the dangerous world mine, from Friday to Friday.'

'You specialize in the Mind?' Mrs Angel asked Dr Apfelbaum.

He nodded.

'Who cares about the Mind?' she went on angrily. 'Can you minister to a decayed body?' – holding out her shrivelled fingers. 'Can you mend these, make them smooth and young again? I'd give my money for that.'

At the word 'money' he stirred, put down his glass, put out his cigarette.

'She's got money,' I whispered, 'more than you'd think.'

He took her shrivelled fingers in his white soft hand and looked at them, like a jeweller looking at a necklace; then put them down. 'I couldn't promise,' he said. 'We're still experimenting, but if you cared to come and see me . . .'

She looked frightened. 'I'm poor,' she whimpered. 'See how poor I am.' She showed him her shabby clothes, her empty purse, her shoes with downtrodden heels.

'As you please,' he shrugged, and gave her his card.

I turned to him eagerly. 'You mean it might be possible – from Friday to Friday, for ever and ever; Sir John for ever tall and with a grey moustache, for ever Leslie to his friends, and I for ever whispering in his ear, "Sir John, dear Sir John, true Sir John." '

We went on to a concert. Dr Apfelbaum said that he loved music. It had been, he said, his great ambition to be a conductor, but this had not been possible. For family reasons it had been necessary for him to take up something more lucrative than music, and so he had taken up medicine, specializing in the Mind. 'I can't say I regret it now,' he said. 'They're not unalike, specializing in the Mind and music – tuning up my patients until they strike a clear true note.'

He sat listening to the concert, lips a little pouting, breath laboured. The music stirred him. He became animal as he

151

listened, eyes inflamed, mouth moist, thick tufts of black hair on his fingers sprouting, like seedlings after rain. Mrs Angel slept, and I looked round eagerly for Sir John; when I had found him, fixed my eyes on his tall figure, remembered he was Leslie to his friends. Thus fortified, I was able to listen unafraid to the music.

When the music was over, Dr Apfelbaum relaxed, his lips dry again and the cloud over his eyes dispelled. 'It's been a lovely concert,' I said. 'Now let's go on somewhere else.'

A taxi carried us past glistening lights. We were swept along, pausing, darting, like a swift river flowing along a rocky bed. I sat between Dr Apfelbaum and Mrs Angel, sometimes swung against one, sometimes against the other. 'How wonderful it is!' I said, excited by the glistening lights, the movement, the confused sound; 'but a little while ago a wilderness, and now – the richness of it! the diversity! welling up like a spring, burning like a flame. Oh Piccadilly, oh Leicester Square, deathless, sublime.'

Dr Apfelbaum was leaning out of the taxi and trying to read a placard. 'New German Move,' he read, and tapped to stop the taxi for a moment, and bought an evening paper. He read it by the beams of light which the street lamps flashed one after the other across our laps. Mrs Angel leant over me to read, too; both of them feasting their eyes on the headlines, forming soundless words with their lips.

'After all, there's nothing new,' Dr Apfelbaum said. 'It was all in the earlier editions.'

'Nothing new,' Mrs Angel echoed miserably.

Even as he said there was nothing new he was turning on to the City Page, running his eye up and down columns of figures, calculating, his lips moist again as they had been when he was listening to the concert, his eyes misted over again. 'Nothing new,' he repeated; 'nothing new at all.'

'Why should you bother to go on experimenting?' I said to Dr Apfelbaum. 'Are not these lights immortal, and these faces, and these sounds? – like dragonflies opening radiant wings for a moment and then falling to the ground, but their buzz ceaseless, their darting back and forth uninterrupted?'

CASHIER

'It's not enough,' Mrs Angel wailed.

'Men must endure their going hence even as their coming hither,' I said. 'Ripeness is all.'

We sat, ripening, beside a dance-floor, mirrors behind and before us, and in them an endless succession of other dance-floors and others ripening beside them. 'Dance, Apple-blossom, dance,' I said. He took a partner, and I watched their sinuous movements, body flattened against body, swaying like a reed in the wind, both their faces (one pale with deep blue shadows, one crimson and gold) indolent, eyelids lowered and mouths drooping.

'You speak with tongues?' I asked Dr Apfelbaum as he rested between one dance and another.

'Perhaps,' he laughed uneasily.

'You're one of the Saints?'

'No, emphatically not,' laughing louder, more mirthlessly.

I burned with impatience for the music to begin again. Why should it stop? If it stopped for long my heart might sink again, leaden and fearful. 'Come!' I shouted. 'Come!' The band looked up questioningly, then nerved themselves to begin again; brandishing their instruments, grimacing. They were wearing loose red shirts with high collars and green sashes, and tasselled velvet caps.

'You must dance too,' Dr Apfelbaum said to me.

I had dreaded this. To watch Dr Apfelbaum dance was one thing, but to dance myself! – that was to put too severe a strain on my new-found happiness, whose roots, striking downwards, might find no sustenance and wither, and branches reaching upwards receive no sap to sustain them. 'No, I think I won't,' I said.

'I insist,' Dr Apfelbaum said, laughing.

Like a swimmer shivering on a river bank, I looked round. 'Come, Mrs Angel,' I said. We stumbled round together. As we danced her bones groaned and rattled. I felt the sharpness of her limbs, and my hand, tenderly clasping her, counted over her ribs. 'Better,' I said, 'than jumping into the Thames from the Embankment. Oh my dear Mrs Angel, I'm so happy.'

She smiled grimly up at me. 'You're young.' It was what she had said on the Embankment.

'When we're happy,' I said, 'there's no youth and age, only life and death. Happiness makes us ageless. We're both alive. See, I embrace you; and in that embrace where's your age and my youth?'

All the while we were dancing, dancing; passing Dr Apfelbaum, trancelike and solemn; passing the band with their red shirts billowing and their green sashes agitated. I stroked her lined cheek and pushed back wisps of hair from her forehead.

'If I were to die now,' she said, 'there'd be life and death, wouldn't there?'

She toppled forward and lay inert in my arms. 'Apple-blossom!' I shouted, still dancing, 'Appleblossom, come and see if she's dead.'

He reluctantly disengaged himself from his partner and came across to where we were. The band stopped, and the other dancers gathered round. 'Steady,' Dr Apfelbaum whispered to me, 'don't let's have a relapse.'

'She said she might die,' I said penitently, 'and I only wanted to make quite sure she wasn't dead. Just to make sure. I thought I'd like an expert opinion.'

He felt her pulse and held a little mirror he carried in his pocket to her lips, and turned back the lids of her eyes. 'She needs fresh air,' he said. 'Let's get her outside.'

I was greatly relieved that she was not dead. Her death would have shattered my happiness – insisting on living when I asked her to die and dying when I asked her to live. We took her into the street, each supporting an arm and trailing her legs behind us. A waiter pursued us, waving a piece of paper in the air, his sallow face anxious and angry, his voice bitter as he shouted to us to stop.

'What is it, Appleblossom?' I asked. 'He welcomed us so cordially, and now – menacing, cruel. What have we done to make him hate us so?'

Dr Apfelbaum's face hardened. 'It's the bill,' he said. 'He can't let us go without paying.'

I was using both my arms now to support Mrs Angel, so I asked Dr Apfelbaum if he would be so kind as to feel in my pocket for some money. He put his hand gingerly in pocket after pocket and found nothing, all the while his expression growing graver. 'Perhaps, after all, she's got some money,' he said, pointing to Mrs Angel's handbag, and looked in it but found only sixpence and a passport. The waiter meanwhile was looking more and more contemptuous and brutal. Despairingly, Dr Apfelbaum went all through my pockets again, and this time in the hip-pocket found what he was looking for – the little envelope I had been given that very afternoon, with three five-pound notes still intact and the change from the fourth. He paid the bill and asked me how much tip he was to give. 'I leave it to you,' I said. He gave a cautious tip, and the waiter scowled. 'More, more,' I said, and he gave more, coin by coin. At each coin the waiter brightened, until he was smiling like when he first welcomed us.

Gradually Mrs Angel revived. She opened her eyes and looked round. 'Has the world ended?' she asked anxiously. I assured her it had not. 'The Niagara Falls are still falling and the Midnight Sun still shedding its light,' I said. She looked relieved.

When Mrs Angel had gone I pressed Dr Apfelbaum to come somewhere else with me. 'It's early yet,' I said, pointing to the undiminished crowds in the streets and the undimmed lights. He looked at his watch, and pursed up his lips, prudent and calculating. 'I've work to do tomorrow,' he said. Patients would be sitting the next morning in his waiting-room as I had, and listening to his coloured birds sing; and he would receive them one after the other, stretch them out on his sofa, listen while they drained off the contents of their minds, head bent sideways, gold fountain-pen ready.

'Work!' I laughed, and took his arm, and led him protesting into a doorway bright with light; felt again in my hip-pocket, paid, and there were new delights arranged for us – on a little stage across intervening darkness a woman dancing. She was dressed in a green star, one point going down between her legs, two points just reaching her breasts, and the other two meeting round her waist. As she danced she sang in a shrill voice about how she went out one morning, and it seemed as though any one of the points of her green star might become unfastened, yet they just held. I longed for her – with one sudden flick the green star removed like a scab, one sudden wrench and her nakedness available. 'Isn't she wonderful,' I whispered to Dr Apfelbaum. He, too, was longing, stirred as at the concert, more deeply stirred, his lips moister, his eyes more clouded, the black hairs on his fingers rich like tropical vegetation. Everyone round me was longing. Our longing filled the little theatre, a great weight of longing hanging over it like a storm cloud. The light went on, and we stood up, dazed and swaying gently to and fro while the orchestra played God Save the King.

'Now I really must go,' Dr Apfelbaum said firmly, and disengaged his arm from mine and made for a bus. I shouted after him despairingly, 'Appleblossom, Appleblossom!' but the red bus bore him relentlessly away, and I was left alone. 'Never mind,' I thought, 'the streets are as crowded as ever.' Were they as crowded as ever? A doubt gnawed at me that there were fewer faces passing mine. I tried to put it away – of course not fewer, innumerable faces, one after the other, innumerable feet beating the pavement. Yet I had at last to admit that the streets were emptying and lights being put out. Soon I might find myself alone and in darkness.

To hearten myself I put my hand in my hip-pocket. Would what I felt there fail me now? I asked myself what I wanted – not to eat, I was replete; not to drink, my thirst had been quenched; not to be carried here and there, I had been here and there; not to hear music, not to dance, not to long across intervening darkness to flick off a green star like a scab. 'What do I want?' I asked myself, clutching flimsy pieces of paper, and imagined a breast – the whole extent of the night, on to which I might lean my head, arms as vast as space enfolding me, tenderness breathing down like sleep.

As I imagined this an arm was slipped into mine. The hand I lovingly guided to join my hand in my hip-pocket. There it also rested, content. Thus cemented together we moved along, occasionally pausing to join our lips too.

26

I Penetrated to the Darkest Corners

I sat in my corner scribbling and no words came, I took up the telephone receiver and no Sir John answered. 'Sir John,' I shouted into the telephone despairingly, 'Sir John, are you there?' and the black receiver pressed to my ear was silent. The life had gone out of it and out of my pencil. My occupation was gone, and on the next Friday when I went to sign the book and get my envelope the clerk who used to give it me, smiling as he handed it, so precious, over the counter, shook his head and sent me empty away.

Now I was an outcast. What taxi now would stop and pick me up? What waiter bring me food? Who cared now to dabble my nails in warm scented water or to shape cloth to my body? I walked, an outcast, along hostile streets, thinking: 'How cruel it is! how unjust! Others possess the dangerous world from Friday to Friday, and I have no part in it.'

I cursed Sir John, Leslie to his friends, but not to me; to me an enemy, his black clothes darkness and his grey moustache ice. He was the cause of my misery, and not only of mine, of others' misery, of all the misery stalking these cruel streets, supplicating these cruel buildings. How powerful he was, bestowing his favours and then withdrawing them, policemen wearing his livery, money his token. 'Down with him!' I thought, 'down with him and his world, burn the ledgers recording his might as title-deeds were burnt by French revolutionaries, break into his palaces – rooms with thick carpets and wide desks and typewriters playing like machine-guns, and destroy! destroy! Track down his hosts of friends and destroy them – the King, the Archbishops, Lords, temporal and spiritual, confidential clerks, commissionaires . . .'

Who were not among his hosts of friends? I paused to wonder. Where could I look for allies? Among the miserable, I thought, and scanned the faces of passers-by for signs of woe, marking them in each passing face – a tall threadbare man with cracked shoes, a wasted woman leaning against a wall and mutely holding out a sprig of lavender, a messenger in a tall hat hugging a black satchel, a Jew with a double-breasted waistcoat searching for a penny to buy a news-paper, a cripple hobbling along on two leather stumps, a woman resplendent, breasts and thighs wrapped in delicate silk, nails and lips glowing fiery. 'We must stand together,' I pleaded. They shook their heads, friends of Sir John, his brothers and sisters.

Lower I must go, I thought, and lower; to the very dregs, shivering unfortunates, homeless and hungry, sitting on public benches and watching pigeons come and go, and turning over crumpled newspaper sheets salvaged from rubbish-bins. I edged on to a crowded bench in a little open space with tall buildings crowded round it. 'Comrades,' I whispered, 'what is it we lack that we have to sit idly here watching these pigeons come and go and turning over these crumpled newspaper sheets?'

'Money,' one answered, and the others echoed: 'Money!' their eyes brightening, their sluggish faces animated.

'After all,' I went on, 'we're human beings like the others with the same needs and appetites. Our lungs work by the same mechanism as theirs, we came into the world in the same way and shall as surely leave it. Why should we be shut out from all that they enjoy? – the music, the warmth, women.'

Again they stirred. 'Yes, why?' one said, and the others echoed: 'Why?'

'There's no reason,' I continued eagerly, 'except our disunity. We're many and they're few; only six of us here on this bench, but everywhere other outcasts. If we stood together, firm, indomitable, what could we not do? – destroy this scheme of things and build it nearer to the heart's desire, tear down this prison in which we're confined, put our gaolers to flight and be free to enjoy the lovely earth, free and happy.'

Their attention had wandered. They were poring over their crumpled newspaper sheets again, watching the pigeons come and go again. 'Leave us alone,' one of them said, and the others echoed: 'Leave us alone!'

I got up and went away. 'I must go still lower,' I thought, and penetrated to the darkest corners, figures huddled under bridges, congealed together in decaying buildings, finding shelter in cold churches, singing, fiddling outside public houses, droning songs against the traffic's roar, hawking flowers or matches, standing placarded with their ills, work-stained, weary, packed in railway carriages, pulling reluctant coins out of worn purses, anxiously eyeing meat where it

hung brightly lighted. These, too, refused to accept me as their champion. 'I am outcast even by the outcast,' I thought. Among all the lights around me there was not one which burned in expectation of my coming, among all the faces not one which lit up at the sight of mine. Not even the shops invited me in, since I had nothing to spend; not even the trams gliding past would pause to let me board them. All this great city, all these multifold activities, yesterday incorporating me, today hostile – why? My hand reached for my hip-pocket and found nothing there. It was empty.

Mrs Angel touched my arm. 'You again?' she said. We walked along together. 'I've been looking all day,' I said, 'for people to join with me in pulling down this cruel city, so full of misery and injustice, tormenting so many, and then rebuilding it nearer to the heart's desire.'

'Whose heart?' she asked.

'Mine,' I said. 'First I'd abolish money.'

She shuddered. 'You'd abolish money. That's what everyone wants – money.'

'I don't care what everyone wants,' I shouted angrily. 'Money is cruel, money breeds hatred and fear, money corrupts and allows the Few to prey on the Many.' I took her hand and said coaxingly: 'Give me some money. Just a little, a few pounds.'

She laughed. 'I thought first of all you meant it – about destroying money. It gave me quite a turn. How could I travel, and see the Midnight Sun and the Niagara Falls if I had no money? Who would bother with me, an old tiresome woman, unless I could pay?'

'I did mean it,' I said. 'I want to abolish money.'

She looked craftily in her purse, muttering: 'I haven't got much with me; only a few shillings.'

'Give me them,' I pleaded.

She counted three shillings into my hand.

27

The Everlasting Pursuit of Money

The three shillings Mrs Angel had counted into my hand were soon spent, so once more I climbed the winding wooden stairway to Wilberforce's office. Wilberforce was reading newspapers one after the other, hurriedly turning over their pages and his eyes pouncing when he saw something that interested him, like a kingfisher pouncing down on a lake. He held out his hand genially: 'I was hearing about you only the other day. Who was it from? Ah yes, I remember. It was from Sir John at a lunch at the London School of Economics. He spoke most appreciatively of you.'

'I've finished with Sir John,' I said bitterly, 'and all he stands for. I'm on *your* side now.'

He looked surprised and rather irritated.

'I want to abolish money,' I went on.

'Of course, I'm with you there,' he said coldly.

'Wilberforce, how's it to be done?'

He pressed the tips of his fingers together like a lawyer considering a complicated case. 'I feel we ought to begin,' he said, 'by some simple measure that won't create panic – by nationalizing the banks, say . . .'

'Wilberforce,' I interrupted, 'lend me five pounds.'

'Then,' he went on, warming, his voice rising and swamping my request, 'we shall be in a position to nationalize the key industries, as mining, steel, textiles, transport.' He had cut himself shaving that morning, and on his neck there was a thin trickle of blood.

'Wilberforce,' I began again, 'lend me . . .' but he broke in relentlessly. 'Having nationalized the key industries we shall be in a position to take over the land, retail trading, secondary industries, until the whole economic machinery of the State is in our hands.' As he talked he walked restlessly over to the little window in his office, next to the one I had looked out of with Miss Annerley. I joined him there, and together we looked down, rain gently washing roofs and chimneys and steeples and far below us the grey pavement. 'Then,' he went on, 'we shall be in a position to do away with exploitation.'

'And money,' I added eagerly.

'And money,' he echoed without enthusiasm. 'Then,' he whispered more to himself than to me, 'we shall be in a position to change men.'

'Wilberforce, how?' I asked, awed, still looking down.

'We'll persuade,' he said, 'we'll educate, we'll demonstrate with facts and with figures.'

I laughed, seeing under the roofs spread out beneath us men clustering round money like ants round a dead rat, sucking sustenance, struggling frenziedly to get near, maddened and exhilarated by the stench, staggering unsteadily away with morsels of flesh.

Wilberforce fell into a rage, his eyes malignant, his fists clenched. 'Very well then, we'll coerce. We'll drive them to their own well-being, if necessary at the end of a gun.'

'That's better,' I said.

'We'll be ruthless,' he raged, 'destroying everything and everyone who impedes. Then,' his face softening, 'at last there'll be freedom and peace and release from the everlasting pursuit of money.'

I took his hand, cold and unresponsive, in mine. 'Let me join you. Shoulder to shoulder we'll stand, comradely, our hearts set on freedom and peace and release from the everlasting pursuit of money. Wilberforce, lend me five pounds.'

He withdrew his hand and filled a pipe. Then deliberately he took out his note-case and extracted a pound and gave it me. It was a final and complete settlement. I should never see him again. 'Received, twenty pieces of silver,' I wrote on a piece of paper, and handed him his receipt.

I sought out all my friends, one after the other. Flavell, his novel about a working-class family finished, was working at Publicity. I waited for him in a long room whose walls were covered with pictures. There was a picture of a woman in shorts and a little white bodice bounding over a meadow, and a picture of a tall man with green hair stepping into a long black car, and a picture of an elderly couple sitting hand in hand looking down on a tennis court, and a picture of a woman in a bathing costume lying in the sun with her arms and legs outspread; many pictures, all of freedom and peace and release from the everlasting pursuit of money. 'You too,' I said to Flavell when he came, taking his arm and walking up and down the room with him and sometimes pausing in front of a picture, 'are with us, with Wilberforce and me, shoulder to shoulder, comradely.'

'What do you want?' he asked anxiously.

'Money,' I answered, standing in front of the picture of a woman in a bathing costume, arms and legs outspread, molten in the sun.

'I'm broke,' he said hoarsely. 'If a few shillings will be any good to you . . .'

'They will, they will,' I said eagerly.

He gave me four shillings.

'Couldn't I have the sixpence too?' I asked humbly, seeing one in his hand.

He gave it me.

Strode I found in his little room overlooking the back of the British Museum. He was sprawling over a typewriter. 'I'm struggling to finish a novel,' he said, looking up at me woefully, 'and I've got stuck. There's a love scene that has to come and I can't write it. Stephen (that's my hero) goes off with Sally. It's all right in the train because they don't get a compartment to themselves, and it's all right on the channel steamer because it's a rough crossing, but now they've arrived at a little hotel in Normandy and taken a room overlooking the sea, and it's a moonlit evening. It can't be postponed any more, and I just can't do it.'

'You haven't grown tired of Love?' I asked accusingly.

He denied indignantly that he had. 'It's not that at all,' he said: 'only that I can't *write* about it any more.'

'Why not slip over to Normandy yourself,' I suggested, 'and see whether you couldn't reproduce the scene. Then you'd be able to describe exactly what happened.'

'Of course, I might go with Edna,' he said doubtfully, sighing, 'but I doubt if it would help. It's not so much this particular novel I'm worrying about,' he went on sadly, 'but the future. How am I to write novels if every time I come to a love scene I get stuck?'

'I got stuck with Sir John in the same way,' I said. 'It's terrible. The only thing to do is to work for freedom and peace and release from the everlasting pursuit of money. That's what Wilberforce and Flavell and I are doing.'

'I agree,' he said eagerly. 'I'm of that way of thinking myself. I wrote a letter about it to the *News Chronicle*. Perhaps you saw it. I felt I must *do* something, however little.'

'You're right,' I said, jumping up. 'Action's the thing. Let's . . . let's write another letter to the *News Chronicle*, now, without any more delay.'

I tore the sheet of paper out of his typewriter, a few lines typed on it – 'Stephen turned away from the window. Sally had begun to unpack her bag. "You've got no doubts," he whispered, "because if you have, even now . . ." ' and inserted another sheet. 'Now,' I said determinedly. 'To the editor, the *News Chronicle*, Sir, we the undersigned, representing all shades of political opinion, feel that the time has come for men and women of goodwill to stop killing each other and preying upon one another. The world, we feel, is a pleasant habitation amply supplied with the wherewithal to satisfy all reasonable human needs. Why, then, should not mankind settle down at last to the quiet enjoyment of that abundance which Nature and their own ingenuity have made available?'

Strode read through what I had written and we both signed it. 'That's that,' I said. 'Now I want to ask you a question. Have you got any money?'

He looked frightened. 'I've got a house in Wimbledon which an aunt left me,' he said. 'It brings in about eighty pounds a year.'

I saw this house with its garden and little porch, one of a row of houses, Strode's. An architect had planned it, brick-layers piled brick on brick, carpenters planed and cut wood to make doors and window frames, plumbers fitted in hidden pipes like intestines. The wood for it had grown in distant forests, the metal for it had been dug out of the earth and smelted in a glowing furnace, trees growing for Strode far away, ore slowly through centuries and centuries depositing itself for Strode, and for him sweat forming on faces splashed with the furnace's glow like tree-trunks with the sun's glow. Then the house finished, all new; then occupied, children washing through it and leaving marks as the tide does, so many people passing the house with a pang because there they had quarrelled and rejoiced and sorrowed, so many more passing it indifferently, one of a row, indistinguishable from the rest, Strode's.

'Give me your house,' I said to Strode.

He got up, agitated. 'No, I couldn't do that. That's out of the question.'

'Give me a little of it,' I pleaded; 'one room, the little attic, or just a door or two, one door, the garden gate.'

He shook his head. 'If you're in need of money I might lend you a little.'

I said that I was in need of money and he gave me two pounds.

From my friends altogether I collected five pounds. It was late when I had finished collecting. There was the money, pieces of paper and coins, which I had earned that day. My hours of work had been long. Other workers had long ago gone home, but I had toiled on and now had my reward — the pieces of paper and coins I held in my hand. What should I do with my five pounds? I wondered, and remembered the pictures in Flavell's gallery each telling me what to do with them; walked up and down the long room where they were hung torn between one picture and another, now pausing in front of the long black car, almost decided, looking furtively out of the corner of my eye at the woman lying with arms and legs outspread in the sun, moving on to her and pausing there, again almost decided, but catching a glimpse of the elderly couple looking down so serenely on their tennis court, until indecision made me frantic, and I rushed furiously from one picture to another, shouting, the pictures becoming distorted, the tall man with green hair menacing, the woman in shorts and a little white bodice wailing for her demon lover as she bounded over the green grass.

I closed my eyes and opened them to see the Thames flowing past, threading its way through London, reflecting lights, receiving sewage, debris, hopeless inert bodies even, bearing these along, yet unpolluted, its source for ever bubbling freshly out of the earth, its mouth for ever emptying into the wide ocean. I decided to let the Thames have my five pounds. The coins were soon lost to sight, a little splash and then swallowed up; the notes bobbed along the surface, my eyes following them. They were my treasure where my heart was. My heart went bobbing along the surface of the Thames towards Gravesend and the wide ocean.

28

Armed with Blood against Death

I dreamed that night of a room in a hospital. There was an acrid smell in the air, and in a bed lay a woman almost dead. Her mouth was drawn, and her eyes, sunk in deep pits, were agonized, like a flame straining not to go out. A shadow seemed to hang over her, advancing, deepening. A doctor took her pulse and smiled reassuringly. Two nurses stood by her bed, and I held her hand, crying and frightened. This was the thing I had known of, talked and thought about, written about – Death, and now that it was near it seemed unfamiliar, as though no one had ever died before and a new horror had revealed itself on earth.

Her hand was cold and inert. I pressed it but there was no answering pressure, like when we had quarrelled and I had tried to make up the quarrel before she was ready. I held her cold inert hand in mine and waited while the grey dawn turned into day, and traffic began to pass outside and shouts to be heard, my mind blank, uncomprehending. All the ebb and flow of passion, hate and love locked together like wrestlers, now one uppermost and now the other; children being born, mine and hers, and quiet evenings, and ecstasy and despair and tedium, and now this grey empty morning when I waited.

'I love you,' I whispered.

She smiled grimly. I did love her. 'Love,' I thought, 'is beyond Love and Hate. Love is beyond Lust.' At that moment when I lusted least I loved most. My love enfolded her, and Lust's whisper – 'Let her die, let her die!' ceased. Lust burnt out to a little heap of grey ash, and Love irradiated all my being. I felt a great tenderness for her wasted body and gaunt struggling face and eyes straining not to go out.

'Now I love you,' I whispered, 'at last.'

She fought against the advancing shadow of Death like a swimmer swimming against the tide. If she ceased fighting for a moment, Death would be upon her and her eyes hold no more light. She mustered up her few remaining energies, beating Death away and then awaiting a new onrush. Alone, she would not have bothered to resist Death. What was life for herself alone? – so many more days followed by nights, so much more happiness followed by misery, so many more winters followed by spring and so many more springs followed by winter, so much momentary satisfaction followed by dissatisfaction, moods coming and going. If she had been alone, she would have thankfully let Death engulf her, an end now instead of hereafter.

I understood that it was because she loved that she fought to live. Her and my children were like veins binding her to the earth and to mankind and to me, and not even Death was strong enough to detach her. Everyone she loved, everyone whose face was familiar to her, all who thought of her tenderly, held her back from Death. All mankind held her back because they were all brothers, one family and she of it.

169

One or two had separated themselves and lain down beside her, but all were brothers, of one parentage, with one destiny, and they, her brothers, wanted her to stay among them.

With difficulty the doctor squeezed a drop of blood from the woman's wasted finger, then a drop of blood from mine. He tested these drops of blood and found they would mix. Then my living arm was laid beside her dying one, and both our arms were pierced and connected by a glass tube. The doctor pumped, and red blood flowed from my arm to hers. I understood that this red blood was life, revivifying, like rain falling on parched earth. The woman's parched veins sucked it up and she gained strength. It flowed between the two of us making us one flesh. Our other unions had been partial, but not this one, with the same blood flowing through our veins, one blood-stream.

Her ashen cheeks gradually flushed. She was armed with blood against Death and Death fled. 'This is my blood, drink this,' I thought, and understood how blood might wash away Death, flow into ashen souls and quicken them. 'The spirit quickeneth,' I thought, 'and blood becomes spirit when it flows into another's veins. Love resolves the ever-lasting conflict – flesh lusting contrary to spirit and spirit lusting contrary to flesh, since Love makes flesh spirit.' My blood, heated so often by tumultuous passions, chilled so often by tumultuous fears, was transubstantiated into a flow of warm revivifying Love. For a moment the veil was lifted and the Mystery became comprehensible. Then I awoke, tremulous again with passions and fears.

29

Oh, Farewell Life!

I felt my appetite to live ebbing and knew that the components of this appetite would drop away like dead petals – my body nevermore reaching after another, fingers nevermore reaching after money; the struggle to force a way through darkness and bewilderment and be defiantly alone, abandoned. It would all soon come to an end and I should close my eyes and be at peace, not needing to summon up my energies to earn or fornicate or relate myself to what was happening in the world, nor to fit myself into any role whatsoever. These activities I might now leave, like a clerk leaving unanswered letters and unbalanced accounts littered about his desk when he goes on holiday. They no longer mattered to me. I was soon to be released from a prison and its routine, and felt accordingly light-hearted, too happy for mortality.

Knowing I should soon die I looked back and saw no beginning to my life and forward and saw no end. I had existed separately for a little while, like a particle of dust drifting into sunlight and momentarily apparent there. My life was not the thirty-three years I had lived, the wear and tear, the success and failure, the happiness and misery, the good and evil of those thirty-three years. All that had happened to me from the moment I was conceived till now, when I knew I was soon to die, so poignant though it had been, so ecstatic and so agonizing, was not the substance of my life. Each event and emotion and mood had been woven into an eternal fabric. My life was part of a Whole comprehending the universe and all therein, comprehending Eternity and Time processing through it; and in relation to this Whole my life had neither beginning nor end, and could not be computed. I saw God counting over the hairs of my head one by one like a pious woman telling her beads, and I saw God looking through immeasurable space at a universe littered with worlds like a sea-shore with grains of sand.

'Soon,' I exulted, 'I shall lust no more.' My soul would rise out of the flesh which had wrapped it round for thirty-three years like a butterfly out of its chrysalis. How grateful I was to this flesh, which had made possible the joy of this moment when I saw that I should soon shed it! How joyous a memory was each of its manifestations, the slightest, the most fantastic, now looked back on, seen as flames darting out of a fire which had to burn to go out. I remembered the first awakening of Lust in me, the terror and exhilaration it aroused; then the separating out of its constituents, all insistent, Flesh thirsting, Mind thirsting, wanting to dominate and be dominated, gorging and retching and gorging again; now a pattern into which everything fitted, precious pattern, final, all-inclusive, now the pattern shattered and again darkness and bewilderment; and sometimes for a moment, oh unforgettable moment! separate thirsts coagulating again into one thirst momentarily quenched, and in that, momentary peace.

On a clear autumn day I set out to make my round of farewells. First I said farewell to the earth. I had walked about this earth for thirty-three years, and should have liked to have left behind me some souvenir of my tenancy, recording the delight I had taken in it. There were streets and fields and rivers I knew, having mixed myself with them. These I bade farewell separately, remembering how I had raged over those flagstones, entered that door expectant, mournfully followed along the course of that river and watched darkness descend on to those fields. I climbed up to a small church on a hill overlooking the sea. By this church one evening I had walked up and down, the air rich and warm, and exulted that I was part of the richness and warmth around me, that I too was ripening towards a harvest.

I went into the church, a little ancient church, now empty, but on Sundays collecting a few men and women and containing their quavering prayers and hymns. The large Bible stood open at the last Sunday's lesson, the altar was tidy, cassocks neatly hanging in their places. This scene also was part of my life, sentences in that opened book haunting my thoughts and desires as no others had. What did I believe about the book and its setting now when I had come to make my farewell? Was this little church which had stood on its hill overlooking the sea for some centuries, receiving the newly born and the newly dead, mumbling its blessing over marriages – was it, like me, soon to die? All that men had ever believed in their long troubled history echoed round me, a confused sound, and all their institutions processed past like a seaside carnival; and I understood that beliefs and institutions were as necessary to mankind as my flesh had been to me, and, like my flesh, necessarily imperfect, capable of only momentary satisfaction, existing in order not to exist. Thus it would always be, I thought – one man reducing the world to the dimensions of a grain of sand and another magnifying a grain of sand to the dimensions of the world, the fiery prophet proclaiming his gospel and the fiery saint renouncing what the fiery sensualist gorged, all expending what had to be expended, until they faltered, felt as I did the appetite to live ebbing, and reluctantly or gladly or indifferently prepared to die.

'Little church on your hill,' I whispered, 'farewell! Perhaps so many years hence you too will be a heap of forgotten stones, or perhaps placarded with ribald insults, a mockery. Perhaps men will bow their heads then before other altars than yours, perhaps not bow their heads at all. Yet for me you have provided a reminder of Eternity, and for that I am grateful; going here and there you have kept alive in me quaveringly a sense that men are brothers and must love one another, and for that I owe you thanks.'

As for the naked earth itself and all its diverse creatures and vegetation – it had nourished me and borne the weight of my body, and would receive my body when there was no more life in it. It had consoled me and exhilarated me and infected me with its savagery and fecundity. Between it and me there was an indissoluble connection, till death parted us. 'Even now,' I thought, 'at this late hour when I know I must soon die, how I should fight for my remaining moments if they were threatened! how easily passion still might stir, trembling, parched, insistent!'

Outside the little church I took up a handful of earth and crumbled it in my hand, and looked round at grass and trees and in the distance the sweeping sea.

Next I said farewell to my wife and children. We had survived, a little unit, like shipwrecked men clinging to a spar in a stormy sea. First two, a man and a woman, impelled to join our bodies together, then the others coming, pushed crying into the world, helpless yet thirstily sucking their milk; on a day smiling, on a day sitting up, standing, tottering a few steps, mouthing broken words. How often we, the two principals, had shouted at one another – 'Out of my sight for ever!' and yet remaining together, growing together like the branches of a tree, swayed and bent by passionate gusts but not cracking. How often we had sat watching logs consume and talking – thus it is with us and thus, thus it might be and thus, shaping our restless desires into abstractions. Now, soon to die, I understood that this talk was nothing, these restless desires and abstractions into which we had shaped them, nothing. Through our agency children had come into the world. Our passion had borne fruit, and this fruit was new life eager to burn itself out, as I had almost burnt myself out. I thought of my children living on after me, following the same vain hopes I had followed, falling into the same despondency and experiencing the same bewilderment. Perhaps they would die on a field of battle, or shed their blood pursuing some ideal to its terrible extreme; perhaps spend themselves in the pursuit of money or knowledge or sensuality or virtue. It seemed then to matter as little as whether they were clever or stupid, short or tall. They existed, they were alive, and that sufficed. 'The only horror,' I thought, 'is sterility, and that soon passes.'

I picked up my children one after the other, so eager, their faces uncreased, their eyes unfearful. In them life began again. It would always begin again, the dry husk falling away and the seed left to send out a new shoot; a spring bubbling up freshly out of the earth, trickling into a river and flowing through plains and cities into the sea.

In a darkening room I sat with my wife. We had made many plans and cancelled many, spoken many words and unspoken many. Even now you might ask, I thought, 'Do you love me still?' and I sit dumb or pour out my dumbness in a flood of words. This question remained unanswered. Long ago when our love was new and in the spring – how easy to answer it then! Then eternity was in your eyes, or so I said, or perhaps neglected to say. Did the years, I wondered, wash away love along with other debris? The years stretched, a grey waste, between the moment when I first entered your body and now when we sat in a darkening room; battling together through those years, acquiring chairs to sit upon, cloth to wrap round our bodies, food to eat, howling out our jealousy, your groans echoing and re-echoing along a hospital corridor, an ebb and flow of pain, while I waited to be shown the wizened piece of flesh, raw from the recent struggle, our passion's trophy; washed apart and together again during those years, never apart, not even when your head or my head lay faithless on another arm, my life and your life inextricably mixed. 'Is that love?' I asked defiantly. 'Take away desire. How soon it withers, sooner than flowers. Tear up the agreement for better or worse. How frail a bond. Banish the Flesh and the World, and still something remains, so that if I heard your voice or you heard mine after aeons of silence there would be a pang no other voice could evoke.'

Now it was finished, my farewells made. How wonderful life seemed, all its horror like blemishes in a loved face; wonderful even in an idiot slobbering and mouthing, in rich lunchers reeling into the sunlight with business to do, in clumsy embraces paid for with money; even in hatred and envy and the disjointed footsteps of elderly barren women waiting for tea. How wonderful life seemed, in its darkest moments, in black despair. Even twisted and forlorn, how wonderful it seemed.

What was there to fear? only that the universe should be drained of love, and that could never happen; only that riches laboriously accumulated should never be squandered, Law laboriously imposed never broken, passion laboriously confined never expended, and that could never happen. The autumn air was full of sounds and sweet airs. I, a man, an atom of love, was soon to die, as every other man and beast and plant and stone, the very universe, must die.